after dark

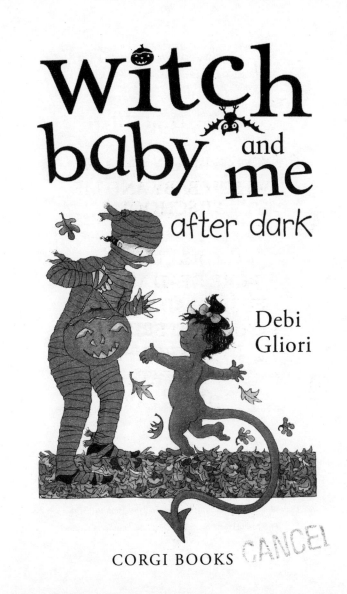

witch
baby and
me
after dark

Debi
Gliori

CORGI BOOKS

WITCH BABY AND ME AFTER DARK
A CORGI BOOK 978 0 552 55678 1

Published in Great Britain by Corgi Books,
an imprint of Random House Children's Books
A Random House Group Company

This edition published 2009

3 5 7 9 10 8 6 4 2

The Random House Group Limited supports the Forest Stewardship Council
(FSC), the leading international forest certification organization.
All our titles that are printed on Greenpeace-approved FSC-certified
paper carry the FSC logo. Our paper procurement policy can be
found at www.rbooks.co.uk/environment.

Mixed Sources
Product group from well-managed
forests and other controlled sources
www.fsc.org Cert no. TT-COC-2139
© 1996 Forest Stewardship Council

Set in Adobe Garamond Pro 14/19.5pt by Falcon Oast Graphic Art Ltd.

Designed by Clair Lansley

Corgi Books are published by Random House Children's Books,
61–63 Uxbridge Road, London W5 5SA

www.kidsatrandomhouse.co.uk
www.rbooks.co.uk

Addresses for companies within The Random House Group Limited
can be found at: www.randomhouse.co.uk/offices.htm

THE RANDOM HOUSE GROUP Limited Reg. No. 954009

A CIP catalogue record for this book is available from the British Library.

Printed and bound in the UK by CPI Bookmarque, Croydon

CONTENTS

Dedicated to devourers of books,
lovers of stories, turners of pages
and especially Readers who
Laugh Out Loud.

WINDING UP THE WITCH

In the hall, a clock chimed five times, paused, and then chimed fifteen times more. Marvellous. It's twenty o'clock – time for supper at Arkon House. This crumbling ruin is home to the Chin, the Nose and the Toad: the legendary **Sisters of HiSS**. In case you haven't already heard of them, you should be warned: the **Sisters of HiSS** are witches. They are very, very old and quite

1

wrinkly. Nobody is quite sure, but it is possible that the Chin, the Nose and the Toad are at *least* four hundred years old. And, as you can imagine, four hundred years of making breakfast, lunch and supper for her Sisters has turned the Toad into a brilliant cook. Lucky **Sisters of HiSS**. Tonight's supper is bound to be *delicious*.

In the kitchen, the Toad is thriftily preparing supper from yesterday's leftovers. At least, that was the plan until she discovered that someone had already been in the fridge and eaten her ingredients. *All* of them. Ten cold roast potatoes, a bowl of orange-and-honey-glazed carrots, three redcurrant jelly vol-au-vents, five slices of rosemary and garlic roast lamb and . . .

'. . . every last DROP of gravy. Drunk. **Gobbled**. **Slurped**. *Gone*,' the Toad moaned. 'For heaven's sake, Nose. Did you have to eat *every*thing?'

Her face hidden behind the newspaper, the Nose blushed.

'And,' the Toad continued, 'you also ate all my lemon meringue pie. Every last crumb of it. I was sooooo looking forward to having it for pudding tonight. It was the best one I've ever made. How *could* you?'

The Nose wriggled uncomfortably in her seat, and from behind the paper came a loud and fruity **belch**. Across the kitchen, the Chin looked up from her computer and Tsssked. 'Dis*gu*sting.'

The Toad slammed the fridge door shut. 'Right,' she said. 'Since *you* ate all the food, Sister dear, *you* can go and pick up some carry-out pizzas for our tea.'

A muffled **squeak** came from behind the newspaper but the Toad was not to be put off. 'And *don't* think we're fooled for one minute

by your pretending to study the paper. We *know* you can't read.' And with one effortless leap, the Toad vaulted onto the table and plucked the newspaper out of the Nose's grasp.

Exposed in mid-gobble, the Nose chewed frantically and tried to pretend she hadn't just been polishing off the last redcurrant jelly vol-au-vent. She blustered, 'Whatever do you mean?' but since her mouth was full of vol-au-vent, all she managed to say was, '**Foff effa oo oo een**!' before spraying the Toad and most of the table with flecks of uneaten puff pastry.

At this, the Chin gave a despairing groan and stood up. She marched across to the table and raked her Sister with a slitty-eyed glare. 'I've a good mind to turn you into a **ssslug**,' she hissed. 'You're a di**ss**grace to the name of Hiss.

We are the **Sisters of HiSS**, not the Piggies of Swill. We are witches, *not* mobile puff-pastry disposal units.'

'I beg your **pffff**,' the Nose tried to say, but the Chin was unstoppable.

She bent down close to the Nose. '**Sssoon** it will be **Halloween**,' she said. 'One of the biggest days in the witchy year. The night when every human child for miles around thinks that all they have to do is slip into a black plastic bin-bag, paint their faces green, hurl talcum powder into their hair and – hey, presto – they're witches.'

'Bless,' sighed the tender-hearted Toad. 'If only it were that simp—'

'The *night*,' the Chin interrupted, 'when *real witches* become so full of magic, they almost *sizzle*. Spells pour from their mouths, their

hearts beat faster and faster, their eyes burn like fire, their hair whips from side to side like a nest of maddened snakes—'

'It's not a good look,' muttered the Toad, but the Chin was deaf to all criticism.

'Sparks fly from their fingertips, they almost *glow* in the dark, and woe betide any feeble human who gets in their way. Woe, woe and thrice wo—'

'Yes, yes, yes,' the Nose hissed impatiently. 'And your point is . . . ?'

The Chin's mouth shrank down to a pucker of exasperation. 'My *point* . . .' she said. 'My point is that *this* year we'll have to keep a lid on **Halloween**. This year we're surrounded by humans. That means we mustn't do *anything* to make them suspect that we are witches. At **Halloween** we will have to stay at home and pretend to be two little old ladies and their pet toad. That means no sparks, no fire, no glowing in the dark and definitely no whippy snake-hair.'

'Tell me this is a wind-up,' the Nose gasped. 'You're joking, right?'

The Chin slowly shook her head. 'No. *No.* *NO*. It's no joking matter. This year' – she took a deep breath – '*this* year, **Halloween** is cancelled.'

One:

A hair-raising bit

I'm staring at my notebook, wishing I could think of a really brilliant idea for a **Halloween** costume. So far, all I've written is:

ghost

dead bride

vampire

mummy

~~*werewolf*~~

~~*witch*~~

Werewolf and *witch* have circles drawn round them because, as my best friend Vivaldi pointed out, we've already *got* one of each of those.

To explain: my baby sister, Daisy, is a **Witch Baby**. That's witch as in: casts spells and will probably sprout chin warts when she's older. As if she can read my mind,* Daisy stands up, scowls at me, mutters, 'No tin watts, Lil-Lil,' before stomping off to fling herself down on the floor beside her dog, WayWoof. She calls her dog WayWoof because she's too little to say **werewolf** properly.

* She *can* read my mind, it's just that she's too wee to understand what it says yet.

WayWoof
rolls over on
her back and
stretches
blissfully,
gives a fifty-
fang yawn

and promptly goes back to sleep again. She does
a lot of sleeping these days, does WayWoof.
Sleeping, eating and growing really fat. Or at
least, her tummy is. The rest of her is normal, if
you can say that about a dog who is

    a) magical

    b) invisible (to everyone except Daisy,
       Vivaldi and me)**

** To explain: Daisy can see WayWoof because it was Daisy who
magicked her into existence. I'm not one hundred per cent sure,
but I *think* Vivaldi and I can see WayWoof because we were both
born under a Blue Moon. Dad says Blue Moons are rare and magical
things, and if you're lucky enough to be born under one, then that
means you can see things that nobody else can. Like WayWoofs, for
instance. But my big brother, Jack, says that's complete rubbish
and a Blue Moon is simply the second moon in a month that has had
one full moon already. Or the fourth full moon in a season with
three full moons. Or . . . Understandably, Vivaldi and I prefer
Dad's explanation. Vivaldi and I are slightly magical — *wee WOO-
HOO* — but nothing *like* as magical as Daisy — *big WOO-HOO*.

c) something my witchy
    baby sister conjured up
Oh yes, and d:
    d) the **smelliest** dog
    imaginable.

Add together a skunk, a gas leak, a decomposing squashed toad and a pile of rotting turnips and you've got

Eau de WayWoof

I wonder if her puppies will smell as bad?

Vivaldi is lying on the floor next to WayWoof, patting her tummy (WayWoof's) and trying to guess how many puppies might be growing in there. Daisy has grown bored of WayWoof-adoration: she has turned herself into a bat and is hanging upside down from the lightshade.

Strange as it may seem, this is what passes for a normal afternoon at my house.

'So,' I groan, '**Halloween**. Help me out here. What can we go as?'

'I like the idea of mummies,' Vivaldi says. 'It's probably pretty easy to do – it won't be difficult to find some old sheets to rip up as bandages, and once we're all wrapped up, nobody will have a clue *who* we are.'

Good point. There's nothing more embarrassing than going round houses at **Halloween**, all dressed up in what you hope is a really nail-bitingly terrifying costume,* only to have adults peering at you and saying, 'Very nice, dear. Lily, isn't it? And what *are* you supposed to be, pet?'

'No wantit be mumma,' Daisy chips in. 'Wantit be pider.'

---

* In Scotland, this is called *guising*. This is short for we-disguise-ourselves-and-perform-in-the-hope-you'll-give-us-sweets-and-money. In America they have something faintly similar called *trick-or-treating*. This is short for we-trick-or-terrify-you-into-giving-us-a-treat-or-else. Not the same thing at all.

I look up. The Daisy-bat is dangling from the ceiling, wings folded across her chest, a determined glint in her beady black eyes. I look down. WayWoof is snoozing on the rug. A bat *and* a WayWoof. Yikes. Daisy is doing *two spells at once.* I wonder if it's the approach of **Halloween** that's making her more powerful.

When Daisy first magicked WayWoof into our lives, I quickly realized how useful she was. (WayWoof, not Daisy.) WayWoof acted like an early-warning, incoming-spell alert. Daisy was just a tiny baby witch, so she could only manage one spell at a time, so when WayWoof started to f a d e away, *that* meant Daisy was about to cast a new spell. Back then, Daisy was a strictly-one-spell-at-a-time Witch Baby. But now my little sister has magically transformed herself into a bat, yet . . . WayWoof is *still there*, still visible, still— **Aaaaagh**. Way*Woof*. **Urrrghhh**. Blissfully unaware that WayWoof has just let rip, Daisy flaps her wings and repeats herself. Somewhat louder.

'NO WANTIT MUMMA. WANTIT PIDER.'

'Cool,' Vivaldi agrees. 'Good plan. Lily and I will

be mummies and you can be the spider from the mummies' tomb.'

I was about to point out that this would mean making a spider costume for Daisy when I remembered. Witch Babies don't need **Halloween** costumes made for them. Witch Babies come as themselves.

Woo-hoo – here comes the REAL THING.

After supper it's time for Vivaldi to go home. She lives at Four Winds, which is a six-and-a-half-minute walk from our house. Normally I'd walk her halfway home, then turn round and come back, but by the end of October it's dark after supper, so Mum gets my big brother, Jack, to be our bodyguard.

She has to ask several times because Jack has his earbuds in.

'Jack?'

Tsss, tsss.

'Would you walk Vivaldi home with Lily?'

Tss, tss, tsss, tss.

'I promised Vivaldi's mum that we'd get her home before eight.'

Tsss. tssss. tsss. tsstssstssst.

'Jack? Oh, for Pete's sake. JACK, TAKE THOSE THINGS OUT OF YOUR EARS AND JOIN THE HUMAN RACE, WOULD YOU?'

'What?' squawks Jack. He hauls out the earbuds and lets them dangle from his collar while he blinks up at Mum as if she's dragged him out of a deep coma. 'Keep your hair on, Mum. Honestly. What is your problem?'

Yikes. Jack is skating on thin ice here. Vivaldi and I pull faces at each other and try to make ourselves invisible. Fortunately Daisy saves the moment.

'Keep you hayon, Mumma,' she cackles, obviously delighted at the idea of Mum *not* keeping her hair on. 'Keep you hayon, Lil-Lil, keep you hayon, Dack—'

'All *right*, Daze, that's enough,' Mum

mutters, turning away to stack plates in the dishwasher.

Which is why she doesn't notice Jack's hair rising up to the ceiling and doing two laps of the lightshade before settling back down on its owner's head. Jack doesn't notice, either because

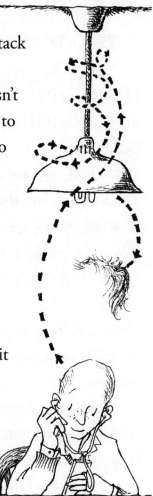

a) Jack never
    notices anything
b) his hair is so short it
    doesn't count
and c) he's got his
    earbuds back in.

Two :

In the wild wood

Walking back through the woods from Vivaldi's house, I'm really glad Jack is with me. As bodyguards go, he doesn't say much,* but he doesn't jump at shadows or get anything like as spooked as I do. Plus, he's got a wind-up torch, whereas I only have a completely rubbish one that *eats* batteries. Talking of which—

Jack stops, gives a huge groan as if he's been mortally wounded and pulls his earbuds out of his ears. This can only mean one thing. His batteries have gone flat. Jack needs to head for the nearest plug socket. At least this way he'll talk to me.

'Jack, d'you know anything about dogs?'

Jack frowns. 'Not a whole lot, Lil. Er.

---

* Apart from *tsss* ~~tsss tsst~~, but that's his earbuds, not him.

They're sort of furry. Leg at each corner—'

'*Jack*. Be serious. I need to find out how long dogs normally take to have puppies.' Although, I remind myself, WayWoof is *nothing* like a normal dog.

'How long? Um. A few months, I think. We can look it up when we get back. Why d'you need to know?'

Oh, boy. You'd never believe me if I told you. I imagine Jack's eyes popping out on springs if I were to explain:

Well, see, our little baby sister . . . I know this sounds insane but – she's actually a witch. No. That's not me calling her names. No. A real witch. Yes. Pointy hats, broomsticks and cauldrons. Yes. Black cats and talking toads. Yes, yes, whatever. Anyway, our dear little Witch Baby has a dog. I know you've never seen her dog. Oh, sigh. That's hardly surprising since she's invisible.

By which time Jack would be backing away from me and hoping that madness wasn't catching. I'll have to make up something to explain why I suddenly need to know how long it takes to grow a litter of puppies. Here goes: 'Er . . . it's an, um, homework thing. We're doing a project at school about puppies.'

I could have saved my breath. Jack isn't listening. He's stopped again and has turned to stare behind him. I turn too, because I can hear something crashing towards us. Something that

is gasping and snorting, louder and louder, as it heads our way. **Aaargh**. What is it? I glance at Jack. He looks every bit as nervous as I feel.

CRASH. Snort, GASP, Snort, **CRASH**.

It's closing in, snapping branches and breathing loudly as it bears down on us. It's far too dark to see properly, but I can almost make out a huge patch of shadow in the trees up ahead. What on earth . . . ?

*

Eyes streaming, covered in thorns and slashed at by vicious branches, the Nose is *not* having a good time. On her way home with an armload of pizzas to appease her sisters, her broomstick gave a hiccup and began zigging and zagging across the sky as if it was determined to unseat its owner. Before the Nose could save herself, the broomstick reversed direction and plunged twigs-first into a bramble thicket.

One minute the Nose was sneakily helping herself to a nibble of the Chin's stringy cheese and pepperoni pizza; the next she found herself upside down and clinging to her broomstick for dear life as it hurtled towards the ground. With a banshee shriek and a loud **snapping** of branches, the Nose and the brambles became one. Some minutes later, punctured by thorns and draped in mozzarella, she **crashed** out of the vicious embrace of the brambles and ran straight across the path of two small humans.

It wasn't until an hour later, when she had reached home and was trying to summon enough strength to pour herself a bath, that it dawned on her exactly *whose* path she'd crossed. *Wait* till she told her Sisters . . .

Three:

WayWoof gone

'She must be maaaaaad,' Jack whispered as the old lady with the big nose blundered off into the darkness. We could still hear her **crashing** and **gasping** through the woods as we turned to go home.

'Mad, bad and dangerous to know,' Jack added, shaking his head in despair at the kind of lunatic who would choose to run blindly through a darkened forest wearing cheese in her hair when she could have been tucked up at home with loud music ~~tsss tssss tssst-ing~~ through her earbuds.

Privately, I thought the old lady with the big nose looked a lot like a teacher Daisy used to have, except it was hard to be sure with all the cheese dripping down from her hair.

We came out of the woods, and up ahead I saw wood-smoke trickling out of the chimney of the Old Station House and Mum's silhouette standing in the window of Daisy's bedroom. As we drew closer, I could see that she had Daisy in her arms and was walking backwards and forwards like she used to do when Daisy was a little waily baby and used to stay up all night.

Jack opened the front door and headed inside on an urgent mission to find a recharger. From upstairs came the sound of Daisy crying. This is not unusual. Bed time is *not* young Daze's favourite time of day. Mum probably didn't know that she likes to have me in bed beside her when I'm reading her story.

Me *in* the bed and WayWoof lying on top of her feet, and—

'Wayyyyyyy my WaAAAAAAWOoo-OOoOOo?' Daisy shrieks from the top of the stairs in tones loud enough to strip paint.

I look up. There she is, my baby sister, all clean and sweet and ready for bed in her rosy pee-jays and . . . bawling her little head off. Mum appears behind her, mouth opening and

closing as if she's trying to say something. She *is* trying to say something; it's just that nobody can hear anything over the din that Daisy, the **Human Shriek Alarm** is making. Dad emerges from the study, his hair sticking up all over like a sea urchin. If anything, he looks even more upset than Daisy.

'Can't hear myself *think*,' he says, taking the stairs two at a time and scooping Daisy up in his arms. 'What's the matter with my little Daisy? You've turned into a banshee baby. *Daisy, Daisy, give it a miss, please do. We're half crazy, having to listen to you.*'

Normally this kind of nonsense calms Daisy down, but not tonight. If anything, Dad is making her worse. *Up* goes the volume, *out* squeeze more tears, and poor Daisy begins to hiccup in between sobs.

'WANTA WAYYYY-*hic*-WAAY-*hic*-WAAY-*hic*-WOO-*hic*-WOO-*hic*-WOOF,' she insists, tears pouring down her face.

I can't take any more. I leap up the stairs three at a time, and when I reach the top, Daisy is already squirming out of Dad's arms to reach me.

She's heavy and very damp from all the crying but she clings to me like a baby barnacle and grabs my face in both her hands to get my full attention before saying, 'WayWoof all gone, Lil-Lil. WayWoof all GAWWWWWWWW,' and then she cries as if her little heart is breaking.

'What *is* she talking

about?' Dad mutters, running his hands through his hair, which makes it stick up even more. 'What on earth is a Waywoo? Lily? Any idea what Daisy means?'

'Er, NO. Not an, um, clue,' I lie, and fortunately Mum and Dad don't see my face flush pink. I *hate* lying, but there's no way I'm about to explain about Daisy's magical, invisible, smelly and currently *missing* dog.

Especially not when the owner of the dog is dissolving right in front of us.

'Let me see if I can cheer Daisy up,' I gasp. I am staggering under her weight, because for some reason babies become heavier when they're miserable. Without waiting for a reply, I haul her backwards into her bedroom, nudging the door shut behind us.

Poor Daisy. I've never seen her *this* sad before. I sit on the bed with her on my lap, wrap my arms around her and rock her gently from side to side. I don't have to say anything. She knows I'm there for her. One hundred per cent. As I rock, I'm trying to find out what's happened, but all poor Daisy can manage to tell me in between sniffles is: 'Spells all boken, Lil-Lil. WayWoo not lissnin.'

Hmm^m. This sounds serious, but it could be that Daisy is too tired to do her WayWoof spell properly, or even that WayWoof, just like a *real* dog, has found something truly fascinating (a rabbit, some juicy bones or a decomposing toad)

and is temporarily deaf to her mistress's summons until she has had a good **sniff**. I've often seen dog owners dangling empty leashes and whistling hopefully for their vanished dogs, so I know that dogs-who-run-away are pretty common. With a bit of luck WayWoof will come back when she's hungry, or tired, or simply decides she's had enough of rabbits, bones or stinky toads.

In the meantime, I'll stay by Daisy's side even if, like now, she's downloaded something truly *evil* into her nappy. **Phwoarrrrr**, Daisy. WayWoof would be proud of you.

Four:

A real hiss

'Oh, how lucky are you?' the Toad sighed enviously. 'The sister *and* brother of our precious Witch Baby. Oh, *when* can we go and see our dear little witch-ette? It's been *ages*.'

'**Pffff**,' muttered the Chin. 'You're sOoOOo soft-hearted, Toad. We don't have to go and visit her *every* day. What's to see? She's still only at the stunted-sprog stage. It'll be *years* before she becomes a proper Sister of Hiss like us.'

'*If* she ever becomes one of us,' the Nose hissed.

'What do you mean, *if*?' the Chin snapped, eyes flashing, hands gripping a teacup so hard her knuckles turned white. 'If?' she repeated, her voice growing shrill. '*IF?*' she shrieked as the

teacup in her hands exploded in a shower of china shards.

Uh-oh, the Toad thought, backing across the kitchen and looking for somewhere to hide. Just in time, she hopped into the relative safety of the dishwasher. It was obvious that the Chin's temper was reaching boiling point.

'We don't do ifs, you idiot!' she roared. 'There *are* no ifs, buts or maybes. No mights, possiblys or perhapses. *Our* **Witch Baby** is

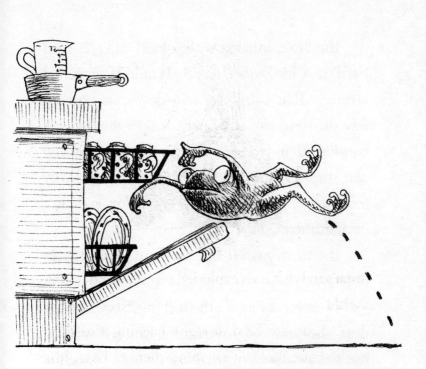

one of us. *We* created her out of the raw material of a human baby. *We* made her into the witch she will become. Without us and our magic, there would *be* no **Witch Baby**. There would only be a run-of-the-mill, bog-standard, one-size-fits-all baby.'

The Nose inhaled with a loud **hiss** and fixed the Chin with a look that could have melted tarmac. 'That baby,' she said slowly, 'is nothing *like* us. Read my cruel narrow lips: that baby is *trouble*. If it were up to me, I'd have already cast the **Diaper of Doom** spell, closely followed by the Nappy of Non-existence enchantment . . .'

The Chin gasped and the Toad gave a **moan** of **terror**.

'N-never *say* such a th-th-thing, **Siss-Sisster** dear,' she quavered, covering her ears as if to block out the awfulness of the Nose's words. Since she was hiding inside the dishwasher, her pleas went unheard.

'You're . . . you're . . .' the Chin managed, her eyes swivelling wildly. 'You're JEALOUS!'

'Am not,' squawked the Nose.

'Are too,' replied the Chin.

'AMN'T, AMN'T, AMN'T!' roared the
Nose, her face rapidly shading from pink to red
to purple.

'Oh, yes you *are*,' the Chin said in an
unbearably smug sing-song voice. 'You're jealous
of Witch Baby because, deep in your little black
heart, you know that she is already a far better
witch than you'll *ever* be. She's only eighteen

moons old and already she's *miles* ahead of you in magical ability. She's already fluent in Advanced Abracadabra while you can barely manage Basic Spelling.'

In the ghastly silence following this, the Toad clasped her webbed hands together and silently rocked backwards and forwards. *Oh dear, oh dear, oh dear*, she thought, cowering in the darkness of the dishwasher.

I really wish you hadn't said that. She jammed her fingers in her ears as she tried to filter out the hisses and **shrieks** and **crashes** and **bangs** coming from outside her hiding place.

CRASH went the teacups, hurled at the wall.

SMASH went the table, upended on the floor.

CLANGGGGGG went the pot rack, flying out of the door.

Finally, disgusted by her Sisters' bad behaviour, the Toad reached round the door of the dishwasher, pressed the 'on' switch and slammed the door shut. *At least this way*, she thought, *I won't have to listen to them fight any more.*

Half an hour later, warm, wet and squeaky-clean, the dishwashed Toad emerged to survey the wreckage. Plaster dust drifted across the ruined kitchen. The floor was littered with broken china and dented saucepans. The table lay like an upturned beetle in the middle of the room. A lesser toad might have burst into tears

at the sight of such destruction, but not the Toad. A tiny smile flitted across her **warty** lips. *HAH!* she thought happily. *My horrible Sisters may have trashed my kitchen, but they didn't find my secret hidden stash of chocolate . . .*

Five:

Demolition howl

I could have sworn that WayWoof would be back next morning, but by the time we had to get ready for school, she still hadn't come home. Mum and I had to practically drag Daisy out of the door to go to playgroup.

Poor Daisy. Her playgroup is next door to my classroom and I find myself holding my breath every time I hear a little one crying. So far, so good. Tears have been shed next door, but none of them by my little sister.

'So – where could Way-Woof have gone?' Vivaldi whispers out of the side of her mouth.

'I wish I knew,'

I mutter as I pretend to write something in my English jotter. I look up, just to check that Mrs McDonald hasn't noticed Vivaldi and me talking in class. Luckily she hasn't, but the dreaded Annabel has. Annabel sits across from Vivaldi and me and is always eavesdropping on our private conversations.

'Where has *who* gone?' she mouths at me, but I pretend not to understand.

'Has she ever disappeared for this long before?' Vivaldi hisses.

'No. Never. And the worst thing is that no matter *what* Daisy does spell-wise, she can't get WayWoof back.'

Annabel is staring at me, frowning in concentration as she tries to work out what I've just said.

'Don't worry. I bet when we go out for **Halloween** tonight, we'll find her,' Vivaldi whispers. 'We'll go round *all* the houses. She's bound to turn up.'

Aaaargh. I haven't made my **Halloween** costume yet. With Daisy being so upset last

night, I forgot to ask Mum if she had an old sheet that I could cut into strips for my mummy costume. I hope there'll be enough time to do this before Vivaldi and I go out. Then I remember it's Vivaldi and me *and* Daisy going out. GULP. Suddenly I've got my fingers and toes tightly crossed that Daisy doesn't become even more weird and witchy because it's **Halloween**. I'm still staring at the wall, imagining Daisy in a variety of embarrassingly weird disguises, when the bell rings for morning break and we herd outside.

'What're you going guising as?' Shane demands, his single eyebrow twitching like a caterpillar in its death throes.

'*We're* having a *Halloween ball* at our house,' Annabel brays. 'Hundreds of people. Daddy says we can stay up as late as we like and I'm going to dress up as Mary Queen of Scots.'

Shane stares at Annabel in disbelief.

'Shut *up*, Annabel,' Jamie, Annabel's big brother, mutters, but it's too late.

'What's Mary Queen of Scots got to do with **Halloween**?' Shane demands.

Annabel heaves a theatrical sigh. 'Don't you know *anything*? Mary Queen of Scots had her head chopped orf.'

'How're you gonny manage that?' Shane

asks,* but Vivaldi interrupts.

'What are you going as, Shane?'

Shane brightens. 'Me 'n' Craig're going as vampires. We've got fangs, fake blood and we'll make cloaks out of black bin-bags.'

Annabel yawns pointedly. Jamie kicks her leg and turns to me.

'Lily? No – don't tell me, let me guess. You'd be great as Morticia Addams or, erm, Marilyn Manson.'

'He's a *bloke*,' Shane mutters scornfully; then, seeing an opportunity for revenge, 'Don't you know *anything*?

* He glares at Annabel as if he'd be only too happy to volunteer to pick up an axe and be her executioner.

Lily's no gonny dress like *him* – are you, eh?'

Oh, boy. Here we go. But before I can say a word, Yoshito says, 'Oh, Lily. You should go as a sea-witch.

Or a *mer-princess*. Or a . . .' Shane snorts, but Yoshito doesn't let him stop her. 'Will you come and visit my house, Lily? When you go out disguising?'

'Me too,' says Vivaldi. 'Can I come and visit you with Lily?'

'Yes,' says Yoshito. 'You are welcome. I am not going out, but I will be dressing up for visitors, so please come and visit Papa and me.'

Poor Yoshito. I'd hate to be stuck inside for **Halloween**, but she seems quite happy to stay at home with her dad.

'Hey, Annabelly,' Craig says, stepping out from behind a tree. 'Fancy inviting a couple of pals to your party?'

Annabel looks as if she's just stood in something a dog threw up, but Craig carries on, 'Shane and me, eh? What a blast that would be. Ah'm sure your daddy wouldn't mind. Whaddya think, Jamie?'

Jamie chokes, **coughs** and seems to be unable to get a word out.

Craig smiles, but his smile doesn't reach

his eyes. 'Course, if there's a problem,' he says, leaning down to put his face next to Annabel's,* 'Shane and me'll just havety gatecrash.'

Annabel rears back as if she's been bitten. She takes a deep breath, fixes Craig with a glare and says firmly, 'I wouldn't do that if I were you. Daddy's hired a security firm to deal with that sort of thing.'

* Which can't be a lot of fun because for such a posh person, Annabel smells** as if she can't afford a toothbrush.

** Annabel still has the wisps of a particularly horrid spell clinging to her. She doesn't know this is a magical pong, and brushes and flosses day and night to rid herself of it.

At this, Jamie's eyes roll so far backwards they look as if they're about to slide down the back of his throat, and Craig is about to explode, but Annabel carries on, oblivious to the fact that all her classmates are beaming drop-dead-Annabel rays at her: 'Daddy takes a very dim view of any **riff-raff** trespassing on our land.'

Oh, for heaven's sake, I think. *Somebody make her* stop *before we all rise up and turn*

her into a nasty stain in the middle of the playground.

'Ewwwwww,' Shane squeals. 'Daddy can just go and take a flying—'

But whatever Shane was about to suggest is drowned out by a banshee howl:

'WAYYYYYYWOoOOOoOO, MY WAAAAAYYYYWOoOoOOoo.'

I spin round, expecting to see Daisy standing behind me, but she isn't there. Again the howl blares across the playground, but this time one of

the panes of glass in the nursery window explodes outwards.

By which time I am halfway across the playground, heading for the nursery in an attempt to stop Daisy howling so much that she flattens the school. Annabel and Jamie's daddy has to hire a team of security guards to guard his home, but we've got something far, far scarier. **Woo-hoo**, that **Witch Baby Demolition Tot**. Don't mess with *her*.

Six:

Big, hairy, venom-dribbling things

It turns out that Miss McPhee, Daisy's play-leader, decided to read her littlies a story at morning break rather than send them outside to play in the cold. How was she to know that *Dogger* (the story of a little boy who loses his beloved toy dog) was *exactly* the wrong book to read to poor Daisy?

As Miss McPhee sweeps up all the broken glass, I try to comfort my sobbing goblin of a little sister. The other playgroup tots are happily hurling sand, water, paint and playdough all about, while Mr Fox, the janitor, hammers a sheet of hardboard over the broken window. When Daisy's howls have dropped to shrieks, then finally ebbed away to hiccuppy sobs, Miss McPhee tries to woo her off my lap.

'But the book has such a happy ending,' she says. 'Look, Daisy. See, on the last page, there's Dogger tucked up in bed with Dave—'

'WAY-*hic*-YYY-*hic*-WoOooO-*hic*.'

'Poor Daisy. I'm *so* sorry you're feeling poorly, pet. D'you think we should give Mummy a ring and see if she'll come and take you home early?'

'Wantawantagohome. Wanta – *hic* – WAYYY -*hic*-WoOoOoO-*hic*.'

Miss McPhee nods. 'Poor wee pet. Perhaps she's coming down with something?'

To herself, Dr Lily diagnoses that the tot is coming down with a bad case of *Missing-my-dog-itis*. To Miss McPhee, I send my sweetest smile. Heavens. If she only knew the real story, she'd probably run out of the school, shrieking even louder than Daisy.

I'm walking home from school with Vivaldi, both of us hoping that Daisy didn't have another fit of the demolition howls after Mum picked her up and took her home.

'My house could be a pile of smoking rubble,' I suggest.

'With your mum standing in the middle of it, wagging her finger at Daisy—'

'Who's still going WAWAWAAAA-AAYYYYWOoOooo.'

'And your brother's sitting in the ruins of your kitchen, eating a bowl of cereal and going—'

'TSSSsssssTSSSssttttSSS!' we yell in unison, then collapse in a giggling heap at the thought of the earbudded Jack, totally oblivious to everything going on around him.

We're still tssstssss-ing faintly at each other and snorting with laughter when we arrive home. Daisy hasn't flattened the house and is sitting in

her highchair, dipping peas in cherry yoghurt*
while Mum is performing brain surgery on a
pumpkin.

Home, sweet home.

The only sheet Mum could spare for tearing
into strips for my mummy wrappings was bright
pink. That's bright pink as in makes-your-
eyeballs-shrivel-up-like-raisins pink. **Ugh**. I'm
going to look like a gift-wrapped maggot.

* Nope. No idea. Best not to ask.

Oh, joy. The only crumb of comfort
I can find is that at least it's going
to be dark when we go out, and
hopefully it won't be too obvious
who exactly is making a complete
fool of herself.

Daisy doesn't think I look
silly, bless her pointy little
head. When I began to wrap my legs in pink
sheet-strips, her eyes grew wide and she toddled
across to stare intently at me.

'What doon, Lil-Lil?'
she breathed.

'I'm dressing up as a silly mummy,' I muttered, tucking a loose strip of pink sheet into my pants.

'Notta silly mumma,' Daisy stated. 'Pretty Lil-Lil. Mummas. Ahhhh.'

Pretty? I don't think so. I look across the room to where Vivaldi's busy wrapping herself in proper *white* sheet-strips like a real Egyptian mummy. She's already bandaged all the way up to her waist, so I'd better get a move on. I grab the remains of my pink sheet and rip it into long raggedy strips. This requires my full attention, which is why I don't notice what Daisy's doing until it's too late.

Oh, *help*. Mum's going to kill me.

'Look, Lil-Lil. Pretty mummas,' and Daisy hands me a pile of perfectly torn strips. Of my bedroom curtains.

Aaaaaaaargh. How did she *do* that? I didn't even see her lips move. Vivaldi has fallen sideways onto my bed, shoulders shaking, clutching her middle as she *whoops* and **gasps** with uncontrollable laughter.

Great. Thanks, guys. Already, this is shaping up to be the worst **Halloween** of my whole life.*

---

* Not entirely true. The real stinker of a Halloween was years ago when we lived in Edinburgh, and Jack took me out guising and we got stuck in a lift between floors at his friend's house. And the lights went out. And Jack's friend decided that this was the perfect moment to regale everyone trapped in the lift with the story of the *Headless Hitch-hiker*. I'm sure that's why I threw up. Nothing to do with all the chocolate I'd been eating earlier on as we went round all the houses. How was I to know that the chocolate had been for all of us, not just me?

I persuade Daisy to undo the curtain-shredding spell, and apart from the fact that the pattern doesn't match up any more, maybe Mum would be unable to tell that my curtains had been torn into strips, jumbled up and then put back together by a toddler. Phew.

'Come on, Daisy,' Vivaldi says. 'Time to get your costume on. What are you going as?'

Daisy heaves a sigh and shakes her head slowly from side to side as if Vivaldi's question was too dumb for words. 'A pider, Valdy.'

Fortunately Vivaldi has heaps of brothers and sisters, so she's used to being sighed at.

'WOW. What kind of spider, Daze?'

'Biiiiiiiiig pider.' Daisy holds out her hands as wide as she can to demonstrate just how enormous her spider will be.

'Biiiiiiiiig HAIRY spider?' Vivaldi enquires.

I shudder. Big hairy spiders are all very well in

nature programmes or in books, but when they appear in your bedroom, I remember that I'm actually a wee bit scared of them.

Obviously Vivaldi doesn't have any problem with giant spiders. In fact, judging by the huge grin spreading across her face, I bet she *was* a spider in a previous life.

'**OoOoOh**,' she gasps. 'Bring it *on*. A big hairy spider dribbling venom down its front and doing that weird sideways scuttle across the floor till it gets to your bed then drags itself up the duvet and vanishes underneath to find your toes and . . .' Vivaldi pauses for effect.

Daisy stares at her, her eyes growing round and wide, and I try my best *not* to think about big hairy spiders cosying up to my bare fee—

'NO WAAAAAANT PIDERS ONNA TOES. WANTIT WAAAAAYYYYWooO-OOooOOOoOOOO.'

Oh, *no*. *WayWoof* was the **Bedroom Guest of Honour with Special Toe-warming Privileges**. Not some hideous, furry, venom-dribbling, creepy-crawling monster of a spider. Oh. dear. Oh. heck. She's off again.

'Wantit – *hic* – wanta – *HIC* – **WAY** – *hic*-**WOOOooooo**.'

Vivaldi looks horrified. 'Oh, *Daisy*, I'm so sorry,' she says, taking a couple of steps towards my sobbing sister. But somehow the bandages on one of her legs have unravelled, and she manages to wrap the trailing bit of cloth round her other foot and—

'Watch out!' she yelps, toppling over and trying to grab something to stop herself falling on top of Daisy. There's a loud **CRACK!** followed by a despairing 'Awww no!' from Vivaldi and . . . there go my curtains again, but this time they're accompanied by the curtain pole, which has snapped in two.

Look on the bright side, though. Daisy isn't crying any more. She's gazing at Vivaldi as if to say, *You know, two minutes ago I could have sworn you were every bit as dull as my big sister, but after that little performance . . . well . . . I'm deeply impressed.*

Seven:

Another hissy fit

'I'm getting a **baaaad** feeling,' the Nose said, laying down her spoon and pushing away her bowl.

'After what you just stuffed down your throat, I'm hardly surprised,' the Chin muttered under her breath. She'd watched as the Nose beasted her way through *three* helpings of spaghetti bolognese, ten slices of garlic bread and two mountainous bowls of apple pie with ice cream. Given how much the Nose had

eaten, it was a miracle that her stomach hadn't exploded. Raising her voice slightly, the Chin said, 'A bad feeling about what, Sister dear?'

'Tonight. *You* know. **Halloween**.' The Nose groaned and licked the last atoms of ice cream from her spoon before continuing, 'Us, stuck inside pretending to be sweet little old ladies while all those horrible little humans are outside, banging on our door and demanding loot. Smelly, rude, stupid little boys and vile, nose-picking, nasty little girls . . . all pretending to be *us*. *US*! The cheek of it! I tell you, Sisters, I won't be able to stop myself from casting a few spells and showing those children that you *never*, never make fun of the Sisters of Hiss. **Pffffffff**. I can barely contain myself. My fingers are fairly **fizz***ing* with magic.' As if to prove her point,

the Nose snapped
her fingers, and
immediately her
hair stood on end
and began to thrash
around her head like a
nest of maddened adders.

'THAT'S ENOUGH!'
roared the Chin. '*Stop* that. You'll get us into
such deep, deep, deep—'

'**poo**,' said the Toad. 'Deep, dark, permanent
poo. Shame on you, Nose. Pull yourself
together. It's only for one night.'

'But . . . but,' whimpered the Nose, 'it's so
hard to keep a lid on all this magical energy.
Especially when children are making fun of
us with their stick-on warts and black plastic
bin-bag cloaks. How *dare* they pretend to
be us? Where's their respect? The temptation to

turn them into **headlice** is . . . is . . . is *irresistible*.'

'Talking of irresistible, how about some biscuits and cheese?' the Toad interrupted, staggering up to the table under the weight of a laden tray. 'Or perhaps, seeing as how it's **Halloween**, as a *Very Special Treat*, you'd like some of my extra-special dark chocolate mints with coffee?' she suggested, placing a heaped plateful within reach of her Sisters.

'**NOOOOOoooooooaaaarghhhh-whynot**,' the Nose managed, unable to resist the golden foil-wrapped sweets. 'Just the one, mind,' she lied, sneakily helping herself to *four* mints.

Wisely, the Toad pretended she hadn't noticed and busied herself with pouring coffee.

'I know this may sound strange to you, my dear Sisters, but I'd be *so* happy to have any children visit us tonight,' she remarked, her large yellow eyes misting over at the thought of welcoming real children into Arkon House.

The Chin and the Nose regarded her in disbelief. How could two witches of such spectacular wickedness possibly be related to this warty sack of tender-hearted *fluffiness*? Surely the Chin and the Nose couldn't be made of the same *stuff** as the Toad? The Chin closed her eyes in anguish as her soft Sister carried on.

'I've already baked some **Halloween** cupcakes, and you probably haven't noticed that I've decorated the hall with bats and webs and giant spiders, and when the dear little children come in out of the cold, I'm going to tell them my favourite **Halloween** joke—'

'ENOUGH!' bawled the Nose. '*You're* the joke. Come *on*. You cannot be serious. Can you imagine the **hoo-hah** if a talking *frog* answered the door? Our secret would be out. Every human for miles around would discover that they had unwittingly been living cheek-by-jowl with three witches—'

'Pretty soon they'd all arrive on our doorstep,' the Chin interrupted. 'With pitchforks—'

'And stakes,' added the Nose.

---

* Stuff: a technical term meaning the atoms and cells from which all life is constructed.

'Trust *you* to think of food at a time like this,' hissed the Chin, her eyes wide with fear. 'I'm talking about being pronged with pitchforks and burned at the stake and all you can think of is filling your fat face.'

'**WHAAAAT**?' shrieked the Nose. 'You foul **hag**. My face *isn't* fat.'

'About the only part of you that isn't,' snapped the Chin, adding cuttingly, 'You porky crone.'

The Toad heaved a huge sigh and began to edge backwards for the safety of the kitchen.

'PORKY CRONE?' yelled the Nose. 'At least I'm not an old, withered, dried-up, **shrivelly**, **DRIBBLY** . . . *PRUNE*.'

The Chin yawned pointedly. 'See? I'm right, as usual. All you ever think about is *food*,' and she shot her Sister a look of triumph before

sitting back to enjoy the sight of
the Nose erupting in a cloud of
steam.

The Toad winced. *Here we go again*, she
thought, measuring the distance between herself
and the sanctuary of the dishwasher. Just as the
Nose brought her arms up into the I-am-about-
to-cast-a-spell-that-will-frizzle-you-like-a-
roasted-sausage position, there came the sound
of the front doorbell ringing.

In the stunned silence following this

interruption, the Toad quietly unwrapped two chocolate mints and jammed them into her mouth. No point in leaving any for neighbours bearing pitchforks and stakes.

Eight:

Of geese and inflatable dogs

'Whose house are you going to first?'

Dad is seeing us off, standing at the end of our garden, his breath wrapping round his head like a misty scarf. **Brrrrr**. It's *freezing* tonight, and there's a full moon rising behind the trees. WayWoof has now been missing for twenty-four hours. Poor WayWoof. She must be *ravenous*. A whole day and night without food won't be good for her or her puppies. No matter how long it takes or how cold we get, we've *got* to find her tonight. Already, Vivaldi and I are shivering in our mummy bandages, but Daisy is snug as a bug in her costume.

Well, it's not exactly a *costume*, but fortunately Mum and Dad and Jack don't know that the youngest MacRae has changed into a

spider. They just think that Vivaldi and I are complete geniuses for making such a good tarantula suit for her.

'So realistic,' Mum sighs in admiration as Daisy scuttles sideways across the lawn. I've got my fingers crossed that Daisy doesn't run up a tree trunk and dangle upside down from a twig. At least, not when Mum, Dad and Jack can see.

'Yeeeeaarrrghhhhh, Daze,' Jack groans, shuddering at the sight of his baby sister dressed up* as a creature that can reliably

---

* Dressed up? That's what *he* thinks . . . heh, heh, mwoah, mwoah, mwoah.

transform my brave big brother into a jelly Jack. He even *takes his earbuds out* in case Daisy tries to sneak up on him; then, with a final shudder, he heads inside to finish his homework. How boring is that? Poor Jack. He says he's too old to go guising this year. Fourteen is too old? Last year, just before we left Edinburgh and moved here, Jack was totally brilliant as the **THING FROM THE BLACK LAGOON**. It was one of the best costumes I've ever seen, but I have to admit it took *for ever* to get all the black treacle out of his hair, and Mum banned us from making Thing-from-the-Black-Lagoon costumes for the rest of time.

Dad shivers and folds his arms round

himself. 'Right, girls. Back here no later than eight thirty or I'll send in the Marines.'

Vivaldi hauls her mobile phone out from under her bandages* and taps on the keypad. 'There,' she says. 'I've set an alarm to go off at seven-thirty and then again at eight. That way we'll know when to start heading home.'

If we haven't **FROZEN** to death first. I'm hugging my pumpkin lantern for warmth, but I'm still chilly. Behind us, the night swallows up my house. Overhead, bare branches **rattle** and **creak** in the wind. And up ahead, its eight furry legs flashing as it scampers through the carpet of fallen leaves, is Daisy, my spider sister.

* Bet the Ancient Egyptians would have loved to own Ancient Mobiles. You can just imagine their texts:

HI TUT I WILL B
2000 YRS L8 4 T
XXX YR MUMMY.

WOO-HOO, here she comes – **Witch Baby**, Queen of Creepy-crawlies. Don't mess with her.

It takes for ever to get to Jamie and Annabel's house. I've never been there before, and neither has Vivaldi. Jamie and Annabel don't have friends home for tea – at least, not friends from school. We pass the gates and trudge up the driveway, wondering when we'll catch sight of the lights of their vast house. I'm assuming it's vast because Annabel has told me at least a million times that it's the biggest for miles around and we've just passed a stone pillar that said:

MISHNISH CASTLE

which sounds a whole lot bigger than a normal house. We walk on, and on . . . and on. Fortunately there are signs everywhere, and some of them help us find our way. Some of the signs aren't all that helpful.

NO
POOR
PEOPLE
Now turn right round
and go back to your hovel

I'm making these up, but there are a lot of these ones:

GANDER SECURITY
DANGER: GUARD DOGS
ARE TRAINED TO
BITE

Vivaldi nudges me and says, 'Don't they mean *Guard Dogs Are Trained to Hiss*?'

At first I have no idea what on earth she's on about, but then the penny drops. *Gander* security should use geese rather than dogs.

'Give me a guard dog any day,' Vivaldi says with a shudder. 'Geese are totally *vicious*.'

Daisy agrees. 'Geeses visses, Lil. VISSES.'

Gulp. If it wasn't for WayWoof, I'd beg Vivaldi to turn back, but we have to look everywhere for our missing dog, so on we go. Past the stables, then the orangery, then along the side of the hothouses and through the walled garden, and finally we turn a corner – and there is the castle.

WOW. It's *enormous*. Annabel wasn't exaggerating. It's the biggest house I've ever seen. Someone has lit hundreds and hundreds of lanterns and arranged them all the way up the steps leading to the colossal front door. There are candles in jars dotted along the edge of a pool of dark water that wraps itself round the castle like a moat. Actually, it probably *is* a moat. **WOW**.

Vivaldi and I stop and stare, but Daisy carries on as if she visits massive castles every day of her life. In fact, she starts *running*, heading for the flight of stone steps that lead up to the front door. For a moment I wonder why she's in such a hurry; then I understand. Faintly, above the noise of the wind, I can

hear a dog barking. Oh, no. Daisy must think
that WayWoof is somewhere inside Mishnish
Castle. When she was younger and could only
manage one spell at a time, finding WayWoof
would have been a no-brainer.

Daisy still a magical spider? No WayWoof, then.

WayWoof around? Daisy not doing a spell at the moment.

But now, with Daisy becoming **Witch Baby Mk. 2** (the hey-I-can-do-two-spells-at-once version), it's all far more complicated.

And now we can hear the little spider calling for her beloved pet: 'Waaaayyyyyy-WoOooOOo?'

And, louder now: WoofWOOoOof ARFWOOOOF YipYipYipYip.

Vivaldi and I are running – running as fast as our mummy wrappings will allow,* but we don't even make it to the bottom of the steps before the front door opens, sending a wedge-shaped blade of light out into the darkness. Silhouetted in the doorway are two huge men, both holding barking dogs on the ends of chains.

* Which isn't very fast at all.

Two men,
four dogs, one
little **Witch Baby**
SPIDER.
GULP.
These men must be
the security guards Annabel
mentioned. They look like giants,
but their dogs look even scarier. Their
teeth glint* in the light from all the candles
on the steps and I don't have to hear their growls
to work out just how mean and vicious they are.

* The dogs' teeth, not the men's.

I can see how hard all four dogs are pulling on their leashes, straining to get up close and personal with this impertinent spider. Oh, *poor* Daisy. She's too young to know that some dogs are really nothing more than people-shredders on legs. I drop my pumpkin lantern and run, desperately trying to reach my baby sister in time to stop something ghastly from happening, when—

The dogs slowly rise up into the air as if somebody has inflated them like balloons. Their leashes are still stretched tight, but now they are straining for the sky. One of the security guards yells, 'Hey, Gonzo! Homer! Stop that. Get *doon*. DOON, BOYS, DOON,' as his feet leave the steps. Then he lets go of the leashes and his two dogs sail off into the night sky, barking enthusiastically. The other two dogs are close behind.

92

'WAY my WAAAAAYYY-WoOoo?' Daisy demands.

The two security guards gape at her. Already confused by the disappearance of their dogs, they appear to be too stunned to do anything about the gatecrashing spider. Then, shaking their heads as if waking from a dream, they step forward, hands outstretched to grab Daisy.

Uh-oh. BAD idea, guys.

'Er – hang *on*!' I squeak, but I'm too late. For a split second all the darkness around Daisy shivers and disintegrates into dazzling splinters of light. What on *earth*? What has Daisy done *now*?

I blink, and there's the **SPIDER**-Daisy at the top of the steps. She turns round and waves her furry legs at us, as if to say, *Oh, come on, do keep up*, then heads into the brightly lit hallway. The security guards have vanished into thin air. There is no sign of them whatsoever. However, there *are* two rather confused-looking geese waddling aimlessly up and down by the stone railings on either side of the stairs – but

. . . surely . . . *no*. No way. Daisy wouldn't have turned the guards into geese . . . would she?

This question will have to remain un-answered for now, because Daisy has spotted a huge oil painting hanging over the fireplace in the hall. Oh, dear. What a dismal picture. It shows a man standing in the rain in the middle of a peat bog with his boot placed on top of an enormous dead stag. Obviously one dead deer wasn't enough for him because there's another slung across the back of his horse.* YeeeeeeUrrrghhhh. And bad as this is, what is really upsetting Daisy isn't the sight of the deer. It's what the deer-killer is holding on the end of a leash.

Yup. A hunting dog that bears an uncanny resemblance to our very own WayWoof. Oh, dear. I look at Daisy. Oh, double dear. Daisy isn't a furry spider any more. Daisy has turned

* How can Jamie and Annabel *bear* to walk past this kind of gore-bath every day? It is so gruesome it's almost scarier than Halloween.

herself back into a little girl. A little girl who looks so woebegone, you'd have to have a heart of stone not to feel really sorry for her.

Ah. Talking of hearts of stone, here comes Annabel, dressed as Mary Queen of Scots, sweeping downstairs in a long white dress. For a split second she looks really lovely; then she opens her mouth and turns back into herself.

'What on *earth* do you think you're playing at?' she demands. 'However did you manage to get past the security guards?' Then, without waiting for an answer, she strides past poor little Daisy and heads for the front door. 'I say. Are those *your* geese?' Annabel's voice climbs higher as she adds, 'They're making the most dreadful mess all over our steps.'

We turn to look. While we've been inside Mishnish Castle, the geese have managed to dump what looks like their entire body weight in goose-poo onto the stone steps and are now busily paddling it underfoot.

'**WOW**. What *huge* birds. I've never seen them before,' Vivaldi says, waggling her eyebrows at me.

'No. *Don't*. I say, knock it orf. *Stop* that!' wails Annabel.

The geese have turned their attention to her and are making little threatening, darting movements at her knees.

'OW!' Annabel yelps, shooing frantically at the geese, but to no avail. The geese are winning. Hissing balefully, the birds are herding Annabel out of her house and backwards down the stone steps.

'AH! OUCH! OOYAH! NO! HELP! DO SOMETHING.'

Luckily, since we're bandaged from head to toe, the geese can't do too much damage to our knees or ankles so we wade in to assist Annabel. Daisy remains indoors, watching from the top

of the steps. I am delighted to see that she has cheered up. This is probably because the geese have taken her mind off WayWoof, even if only for a little while.

Eventually Vivaldi and I manage to persuade the geese to leave Annabel alone and waddle off down the drive, away from Mishnish Castle. Presumably in search of the guard dogs that Daisy turned into balloons . . .

'Well, yes. Ah, um . . .' Annabel seems incapable of telling us how hugely grateful she is to us for saving her from the geese – or indeed, how to get rid of us, since she's obviously *not* going to invite us to her party.

'OK,' Vivaldi says. 'Here's what we do. We tell you a joke or two, Daisy sings a song, you give us some sweets, some money and anything else you can think of, and in return we promise to go away.'

Annabel blinks, but before she can make even a squeak of protest, Vivaldi begins.

'*Who did the ghost invite to her party?*'

Annabel frowns. 'Er . . . hang on . . .'

'*Anyone she could dig up,*' I say, and Daisy, bless her, joins in with a loud, 'TA-DAAAAAA!'

What a *team*. By the time we leave, Annabel has several jokes to tell the guests at her party, and we now have six chocolate champagne truffles, two packets of sweet chilli-flavour crisps, *three* pound coins and a furry toy dog with one leg missing because it turns out that Annabel's heart isn't entirely made of stone.

Nine:

My demon sister

'Hello? Miss Chin? It is I, your good friend Hare.'

Silence greeted Mr Harukashi, friend to the Hisses* and daddy to Yoshito.

'Miss Chin, I am standing on your doorstep, waiting to invite you to a little party I am having tonight. You will be the guest of honour, if you would be so kind as to open your door?'

* Even if the Hisses don't think so. Poor Hare has no idea what he's dealing with. He doesn't realize that his new neighbours, the two helpless old ladies with their pet frog, are actually three wicked witches.

Leaves swirled around Hare's ankles, and the moonshadows of branches looked like the fingers of giant skeletons clawing at the silent door of Arkon House. A lesser man would have given up and gone home, but not Hare. Hare was deeply, fatally, madly, insanely *in love* with the Chin,* and thus was prepared to stand on his beloved's doorstep for as long as it took for her to relent and open the door. Hare was almost one hundred per cent positive that the Hisses were at home, because when the wind dropped, he could sometimes hear little whispery sounds coming from the other side of the door.

Hare sighed and turned the collar of his coat up against the cold. So *shy*, his beloved Miss Chin. Just like his dearest only child, Yoshi.

* I can hear you gasp, 'Is he insane? Can't he see that the Chin has a chin as sharp as a breadknife, and a nature to match? Doesn't he realize that the Chin is hundreds of years old? Can't he see that she is so ugly she makes mirrors smash? What is wrong with Hare that he cannot see the Chin for what she really is?'

To which the only answer has to be: 'Love is blind. Hare loves Miss Chin and there is nothing that anyone can do to change that.'

They'd be sure to get on famously if only he could persuade Miss Chin to be his guest tonight . . .

'*You* answer it,' the Nose sniggered. 'It's you he wants to see. **Ooooh, hoo hooo. TEE HEEE HEE** . . .' She staggered away from the front door, overcome with mirth. The *idea* of her ugly Sister becoming the pin-up witch of this ridiculous little man . . . **Oh, HEE HEEE, TEE HEE HEE.**

The Chin gritted her teeth. *Really*. This was insufferable. That pesky Nose was behaving like

an idiotic giggly
schoolgirl. So
undignified.
And as for the
Toad . . .

The Toad
was squatting
on the doormat,
gazing up at her
Sister with liquid eyes,
her webbed fingers clasping and
unclasping as if in prayer.

'Oh pleeeeeeease. Can I
be first bridesmaid?' she
whispered, a look of such
longing passing across
her warty face that
the Chin wanted to
scream out lOUD,

but of course she couldn't do that, because *then* that infuriating Mr Harukashi would know that she was there, on the other side of the door.

'I know you're there, dear lady,' Mr Harukashi breathed through the keyhole. 'I know you're there, on the other side of the door.'

The Chin stuffed her hands into her mouth to stifle a **yelp**. *How* could he know?

'I know what you're thinking, dearest Miss Chin,' Hare confessed, leaning his forehead against the door. 'You're wishing I would go away and leave you alone—'

The Chin rolled her eyes. This was beyond a joke. How could this persistent little human possibly read her mind?

'So romantic,' the Toad whispered, wiping a tear from her eye. Another tear rolled down her face and plopped onto the doormat.

From the other side of the hall, the Nose sniffed. What a lot of *tosh*. What a pile of ridiculous *fiffle-faffle*. What a pair of *soggy*, *sloppy*, **marshmallowy** *fluff*-brains her Sisters were becoming. If it was up to *her*, she'd have turned Mr Harukashi into a prawn a long time ago. She stifled a little voice coming from somewhere deep inside her that said, *You're just jealous, you crabbit old sourpuss,* then flung open the door to the hall cupboard, picked up a vast china trophy,* held it over her head, winked at the Chin . . . and deliberately hurled the trophy onto the floor.

Now someone would have to answer the door.

* The hall cupboard at
Arkon House is piled to
the ceiling with stuff
that the Hisses cannot
bear to look at, but are
unable to throw out. Old
bristle-less brooms and dented
pointy hats are crammed in beside
rusted cauldrons, cracked crystal
balls and chewed wands.
The vast china trophy is a piece of
ceramic nastiness and was won by the Nose
when she came second in the South-western
Soot-sweeping and Chimney-scaling
Competition of 1827.

We are standing outside Vivaldi's house, arguing with Daisy. It's even more freezing cold than it was when we left my house, and to my horror, I discover that not only did I leave my pumpkin lantern in Annabel's garden, but at some point between Mishnish Castle and Four Winds, Daisy has turned herself into a SMALL **DEMON**. A SMALL naked **DEMON**.

She is bright red all over and is wearing nothing warmer than a pair of horns and a forked tail.

'Come on, Daze,' I try to reason with her. 'Why not turn yourself into something *warm*?'

Daisy merely rolls her red eyes and flicks her tail at me.

'At least she's not crying,' Vivaldi hisses in my ear. 'And besides, if she gets too cold, she'll soon change into something different.'

I don't reply because all of a sudden I can smell a familiar whiff of cabbages and rotting fish; a dustbinny, gassy stench that can only be the perfume of . . . WayWoof!

Brilliant. WayWoof must be in Vivaldi's house. I sneak a glance at the Daisy demon, wondering if she's noticed the smell, but she's humming to herself as she winds her tail round and round her arm.

'Ready?' Vivaldi opens the door and we pile inside, picking our way through shoes, roller blades, pushchairs, school bags and all the stuff that Vivaldi's family keep in their hallway. They are in the kitchen when we arrive, having supper by the light of several pumpkin lanterns. The twins, Mull and Skye, are banging their bowls on the table as if they can't wait to be fed; Brahms, the baby, is fast asleep in his high-chair, and the only one missing is Mozart, Vivaldi's little sister, who has gone to a **Halloween** party in the village. Vivaldi's mum is dishing out pasta, while Vivaldi's dad is spooning it into the twins as fast as he can. The

twins flap their hands and crow with delight when they catch sight of Daisy the Demon, who leaps and spins, her tail spooling out behind her like the tail of a kite. Daisy *loves* this. She adores being the centre of attention, and while she is doing a **DEMON-DANCE** that makes the twins almost choke on their supper, I seize my chance.

'Can you smell that?' I whisper to Vivaldi.

'What – that dreadful *stink*?'

'Yes! It's WayWoof. She must be somewhere in your house.'

Vivaldi is just about to reply when Mull slides off his seat, trailing spaghetti behind him, and toddles over to stare at us. The closer he gets, the worse the smell becomes. Either WayWoof is just about to appear right under my *nose*, or . . .

'*Mull*. Is that you?' Vivaldi groans, adding,

'Eeughhhhh. What have you *done* in your nappy?'

There are some questions that you really don't want to know the answer to. Vivaldi's dad heaves a sigh, mutters something about it being his turn and hauls his smelly little boy off to the bathroom. Poor Mull. Poor Daisy too. I was so sure WayWoof was about to appear, a big pink grin smeared across her face, her teeth sunk into something horrible she'd stolen from a dustbin somewhere . . . Oh, WayWoof. Where have you *gone*?

'Amazing costumes, girls,' Vivaldi's mum says, scraping spaghetti off Skye's chin and re-inserting it in her open mouth.

Daisy has finally stopped leaping around and is standing in front of the huge fish tank Vivaldi's family have in their kitchen. 'OₒₒₒOₒₒ, fisses,' she breathes. 'Lookit fisses,

113

Lil-Lil. No tuts fisses.'

I'm torn between checking that Daisy sticks to her own rules and *doesn't* touch the fishes, and making an attempt to distract Vivaldi's mum from realizing just how amazing our costumes* really are.

'Oh, Vivaldi, d'you remember the devil costume I made for you when you were still at nursery?'

* Well, Daisy's costume really.

Vivaldi groans, 'Mu-u-u-u-m,' but her mum turns to me and carries on happily, 'Oh, she looked so *sweet*. I made her a tiny little red jumpsuit and painted all the bits of her that stuck out with red stage make-up . . .' Vivaldi doesn't need any red make-up now; she is beet-red with embarrassment as her mum keeps going,  seemingly unstoppable. 'But her horns and tail kept on falling off.'

Then, abruptly, Vivaldi's mum stops spooning spaghetti into Skye and stands up.

Uh-oh.

'Can I have a wee look, Daisy?' she says. 'Can I see how your horns are held in place?'

Aaaaargh. Vivaldi and I lock eyeballs in utter **HORROR**. *Help*. We have to stop this horn-investigation *right now*, before Vivaldi's mum finds out that Daisy's costume is the Real Thing. Then Vivaldi's dad comes back into the kitchen, yawning widely.

'Poor Mull,' he says. 'He's gone to bed. Poor little chap is just dog-tired.'

Daisy spins round, fish tank forgotten, her bottom lip popping out in warning. 'Way is dog-tired?' she demands, pushing past Vivaldi's mum and heading for the kitchen door. 'WAY gone, dog-tired?

'WAYYYYWooOoOoOoooOoOOOOO?'

Oh, good *grief*. Within seconds, Daisy's wails set off first Skye, then baby Brahms, and suddenly the kitchen is full of sobbing tots.

'WAY-*hic*-WAY-*hic*-WoOooO.'

'Wah, *wah*, wah, *wah*, wah, *wah*.'

'Bwaaaaaaaaaaaaaaaaaaa.'

Vivaldi's mum sits back down rapidly, and resumes spaghetti-spooning. Vivaldi's dad goes to find some treats for the Guisers Who Made the Littlies Weep, and in the blink of an eye we're back outside in the darkness once more.

Phew. *That* was a narrow squeak.

Ten:

Your personal maggot

Waving goodbye from the door of Arkon House, the Nose forced herself to keep a smile on her face until Mr Harukashi's car was safely out of sight. In the front passenger seat sat the Chin, wearing the expression of someone about to place her neck under a guillotine. All her cries of protest were to no avail. Every excuse she invented to explain why she couldn't *possibly* be Mr Harukashi's guest of honour was swept away by Hare's determination that she should come to his house tonight.

In vain she insisted, 'I have to wash my hair,'

only to have
Hare counter
with, 'Dear lady,
you are perfect just
the way you are.'

Then the Chin tried,
'Tuesday! **Gosh**! That's
my night for . . . um . . . violin lessons.'

Hare beamed. 'You play violin? I too play a little. We will play duets together.'

In utter desperation, out of earshot of her sisters, the Chin looked Hare straight in the eye and **hissed**, 'Listen, mister. I'm over four hundred years old, I'm a **witch**, and if you insist on continuing with this ridiculous courtship, I'll be forced to turn you into a maggot.'

Hare burst out laughing, then took both of the Chin's hands in his and said, 'Hush,

119

dearest lady. I do not understand your strange Scottish customs, but if you wish me to be your maggot . . . I would be honoured. I will try to be the very best maggot you have ever seen.'

The Chin's jaw dropped in disbelief. *Never*, in all her four hundred or so years, had she ever met anyone like Mr Harukashi. *For spawn's sake,* she thought, *is this human completely insane?*

'Your coat, dear Miss Chin.'

In a daze, the Chin allowed herself to be coated, booted, hatted and accompanied out to Hare's car, where she was placed carefully in the passenger seat and belted in.

As Arkon House was swallowed up by darkness in the rear-view mirror, the Chin wondered just what exactly she'd let herself in for.

As Mr Harukashi's car disappeared into the night, the Nose slammed the front door shut and spun round to skewer the Toad with a glare. The smile she'd managed to keep on her face to fool Mr Harukashi had been wiped away. Now the Nose looked like a *real **witch***. Her hair began to thrash and flail around her head, her hands twitched and sparks flew from her

fingertips. To her horror, the Toad realized that at **Halloween**, without the Chin's help, there was little she could do on her own to calm the Nose down.

'Right, **Sissss**ter dearest,' the Nose hissed. 'Let's get ready to entertain these precious little children you're **ssss**o fond of . . . hmmm? Turn the oven on to "high".'

The Toad **gulped**. 'Ov-ov-oven?' she quavered. 'B-b-but we've already had sup-sup-supper.'

The Nose frowned. 'Supper? Whatever are you on about, Toad?'

'**Er. Um. Ahhh**,' the Toad bleated. 'You remember? Spaghetti bolognese, garlic bread, apple pie and ice cream?' *Not to mention the four dark chocolate mints you hoovered down, you greedy pig*, she added under her breath.

The Nose swooped down and put her face close to the Toad's. 'I **asss**ked you,' she spat, 'to put the oven on to "high", *not* to reel off a menu, you cretinous **wart-sack**. Now do as I say or there will be trouble,' and breathing heavily, she waddled through to the living room.

Seconds later the Toad heard the sofa springs **twang** in protest as the Nose flung herself down in front of the television. Soon the theme music

from one of the Nose's favourite programmes could be heard drifting out from behind the living-room door.

The Toad remained in the hall, unable to decide what to do next. If she ignored the Nose and didn't turn the oven up to 'high', her Sister would be furious. There would be **screamies** and **stampies** and it was entirely possible that the Toad's kitchen would be trashed (again). On the other hand, what did the Nose need the oven *for*? After all, she couldn't even boil an egg, so why her sudden interest in the oven? And why did she want it turned up to 'high'? 'High' was for roasting things. Things like potatoes, or chicken . . . or chil . . . chil . . . The Toad's breath caught in her throat.

'Do we have any rosemary?' the Nose demanded, appearing behind the Toad and causing her to jump.

'Rose – rose-m-m-mary?' squeaked the Toad. 'Um. Yes. Ah. In the g-g-garden. Erm. Why do you ask?'

'Is that oven turned up yet or do I have to do everything myself?' the Nose snapped, heading for the kitchen. '*I'll* do the blooming oven. *You* get the rosemary. Understood?'

'Um . . . ah . . . yes . . . that is to say . . .' the Toad gasped, then, catching sight of the Nose's expression, she uttered a squeak of terror and yelped, 'Yes! Right away. Rosemary, here I come.'

It wasn't until she found herself standing under the rosemary bush that she realized two things. *One*: she'd completely forgotten to bring scissors, a knife, a saw – *anything* to cut a sprig of the herb – and *two*: she could hear the sound of approaching voices. Children's voices. Fifteen minutes ago the Toad would

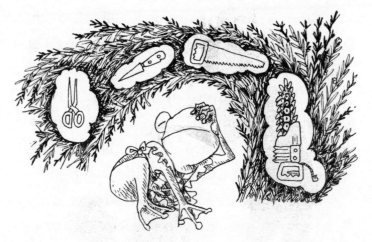

have been delighted to hear the sound of small people coming up the drive. Now, with the Nose demanding to have the oven on high and her sudden desire for the herb most often used to garnish roast meat . . .

Try as she might, the Toad was unable to dispel the ghastly image of her Sister shepherding little children into the kitchen and pausing to sprinkle them with rosemary before popping them straight into the hot oven. The Toad gave

a moan of terror. This *couldn't* be allowed to happen. The **Sisters of Hiss** were trying to *avoid* discovery, not doing something so awful that it would alert the entire population of Scotland to the fact that there were three witches living at Arkon House. No, **no**, **no**. Roasting children was all *wrong*. Somehow, the Toad had to stop her Sister's awful plan from succeeding.

DO something, the Toad told herself. *Don't just squat there, DO something.*

Eleven:

Go on, I dare you

It had been Craig's idea to go guising. It had been his idea to try to gate-crash Annabel and Jamie's posh party as well. *And* go bang on the door of the *Haunted House*. Craig was crazy, Shane decided. At school he was always getting into trouble with Mrs McDonald, but no matter what she said, Craig just carried on as if he hadn't heard. He was fearless as well, which was great sometimes, but far more often meant that both of them landed in deep **poo** because he just didn't have the sense to know when to quit.

Like now, for instance.

Somehow Craig had managed to miss a turning in the dark, and for a while they'd been well and truly lost, stumbling blindly through endless trees with their hands outstretched to protect their faces. After what felt like hours of staggering about, they'd seen dim lights up ahead and realized that they weren't really lost after all. Shane decided that thinking you were lost was nothing like as bad as not being able to see properly in the dark. The second they had wandered out into the woods beyond the lights of the estate where Craig and he lived, it had become dead *creepy*. As his foot slipped in something slimy that he couldn't see, Shane decided he really, really *hated* the countryside. Not only was it dark and slimy, but being out *in* it made him feel like he was the last person left alive. Where was everyone? What kind of people

were mad enough to want to live out here?

The woods were thick with shadows and there were **weird** rustling noises coming from all around. It was freezing cold and the wind plucked at their stupid bin-bag wings and made them flap and slap in their faces. To take their minds off how much fun they *weren't* having, they began daring each other to be the first one to march right up to the front door of the next house, bang on the letterbox and wait to see who answered the door. To Shane's horror, he realized that the next house was the one everyone called the **Haunted House**.

That was when a little voice whispered inside Shane's head – *What if it really is haunted? Then what're you going to do? Run? Ghosts can run faster. Scream? Who d'you think would hear you, stuck out here in the back of beyond?* And all the time this little voice was whispering inside Shane's head, his feet were carrying him closer and closer to the object of his fears.

Up ahead, Arkon House loomed threateningly, its jagged silhouette like a vast **gash** torn in the sky. Slipping through a hole in the surrounding fence, Craig and Shane found themselves walking on tiptoe as they approached the front door. Off to one side, an enormous pit opened up, full to the brim with glittering black liquid.

'Wh-wh-whassat?' Shane squeaked, clutching at Craig's arm.

Craig shook him off and hissed, 'Shut up. It's a swimming pool. Come *on*. Quit being such a wuss.'

Shane winced. The *last* thing he wanted Craig to call him was a wuss. Somehow he had to salvage his pride, pull himself together and show Craig that he, Shane, was braver than a . . . braver than a . . . Seeking inspiration, Shane looked up at the moon.

And *that* was the moment when the Toad launched herself out of a tree and dropped straight onto Shane's upturned face.

'We have to go and check out Arkon House,' Vivaldi says, adding, '*You* know why. Because *Double-U, Double-U, the Smelly One* might be there.'

We're both trying to avoid saying WayWoof's name since Daisy dissolves into a little puddle of woe if anything reminds her of her lost pet. But do we really *have* to go to Arkon House? Surely WayWoof wouldn't have gone there? I can't think of any reason why a dog (even an invisible one) would want to visit a *creepy* old house like that. **Brrrrrrr.** It gives me goose pimples just thinking about it.

Daisy seems to share my lack of enthusiasm for visiting whoever lives there. She's slowed down and is now dragging way behind Vivaldi and me, muttering to herself.

'I can't smell our *four-footed friend*,' I say to Vivaldi.

'That doesn't mean anything,' she replies. 'If our *canine companion* is inside Arkon House we wouldn't be able to smell her from out here.'

'Who d'you think actually lives there?' I'm whispering now, because I'm feeling more and more nervous the closer we get to Arkon House's front door. My stomach is acting like it's falling off a cliff, my tongue feels like a shrivelled bit of ham and my lungs can barely drag in enough oxygen to keep me alive. I'm on the point of grabbing Vivaldi's arm and begging her to turn round and call off the search for WayWoof when we hear a ghastly scream from up ahead.

'YAAAAAAAAAAA. Craig, man, get it OFF MEEEEEEEeeeeEe.'

And another voice yelling, 'Get *away*

from me, you freak. Gawn, Shane. Get away from me.'

Craig? Shane? Vivaldi and I stop in our tracks. Daisy catches up and peers round my legs, obviously reluctant to find out what lies up ahead.

'HELLLP. URRRRGGGGHH-HHHHH. It's got its *feelers* up ma *NOSE*.'

There's the sound of footsteps and Craig appears, running flat out to get away from whatever is attacking Shane. He doesn't stop when he sees us, just flaps his bin-bag wings and dodges past into the trees.

There's a **crash**, a howl, and I see him stumble back onto the path, half stunned and staggering from side to side. What an idiot. He must have run straight into a tree. I'd feel a lot sorrier for him if he hadn't abandoned poor Shane to the *Thing in the Darkness*.

Help. Whatever it is, it sounds *awful*.

'NAWWWWWWW. Get OFFFFFF. Yeurrrrchhhhh. Eughhhhh.' And then, suddenly, Shane appears up ahead. He looks completely normal, which is very surprising, considering the fuss he's just been making. I'd been expecting lakes of blood, buckets of gore, missing limbs and eyeballs hanging halfway down his face; but apart from looking a bit wild-eyed, with his hair sticking up like a hedgehog, Shane looks perfectly OK.

He also ignores us completely and strides over to where his friend Craig is sitting dazed at the foot of a tree.

'Thanks a million for all your help back there, you big creep,' he yells.

Craig rubs his head and groans. 'Aw, come on, Shane. I had no idea what the heck that thing was on your face. For all I knew it was gonny eat me next . . .'

At this feeble excuse, Shane screws up his face like he's just bit into a lemon. I can't say I blame him. Friends are supposed to stick together through thick and thin, not run off at the first sign of trouble.

'What *was* that thing, anyway?' Craig mumbles, getting up somewhat unsteadily, still clinging to the tree for balance.

'No idea,' Shane mutters, rubbing his face as if he's trying to wipe off the memory. He stares at his faithless friend, and then suddenly his expression changes into one of utter terror. He begins to back away from Craig, holding his hands out in front of him as if to ward something off . . .

'What?' Craig demands. 'What *is* it noo?'

Shane appears to be barely able to get the words out: 'Ohhhh, man – it's . . . it's on your . . . your – eughhhhh, *horrible* – aw **noOoO** . . .' He runs off as fast as he can.

'WHAT?' Craig yells. 'What *is* it? What're you talking about? What's going on?' And he turns to look at Vivaldi.

She stares at him as if she can't believe her eyes and gasps, '**Ohhhhh**, **NO**. That's *hideous*. Oh, you poor thing—'

With a shriek, Craig starts beating at himself with his hands, trying to get rid of . . . what? I can't see *anything*. I look at Vivaldi – *what's going on?* – but she has her hands over her mouth and her shoulders are shaking while Craig is doing the full-on Dance of Doom in between screams and howls of 'Geddit off me!

YEEEurchhhhh! Get off me! **HELP**!'

Up ahead, Shane is no longer running and has turned back to watch the show. It's a few minutes before Craig works out that he's the victim of a wind-up. With a blood-curdling **yell**, he takes off after Shane, vowing revenge.

Vivaldi rolls her eyes and turns to me, then frowns. 'Where's Daisy?' she asks.

I turn round, sure that my little demon-Daisy is right behind me, but she isn't. Behind us are the dark, dark woods. Up ahead are the dim lights of Arkon House. There's no sign of a SMALL red **DEMON** anywhere. Vivaldi and I stare at each other in horror. This is as bad as it can get. In our search to find the invisible dog, we've *lost* the baby.

'You go on,' Vivaldi says. 'I'll go back and look in the woods. Don't panic, Lil, she can't have gone far.' And without waiting for my reply, she heads off, back the way we've just come. Up ahead, the lights of Arkon House flicker through the trees. Has Daisy gone there on her own? Has she spotted WayWoof and gone haring off to find her?

'Daiseeeeeeeee?' I call. 'Are you there? DAAAAAAAZE?' I'm running now, heading for the *Haunted House*. Oh, Daisy, where *are* you?

Twelve:

A bolt from the boo

The Toad was delighted with how well her save-the-dear-little-children-from-being-roasted-with-rosemary-in-a-'high'-oven plan had gone. Admittedly, the child whose face she'd landed on wasn't even remotely grateful for being saved, but no matter. Sliding down the trunk of the tree she'd leaped into to escape the graceless boy, the Toad began to hop back to Arkon House. So pleased was she with her own cleverness that she didn't notice the red imp until it was too late.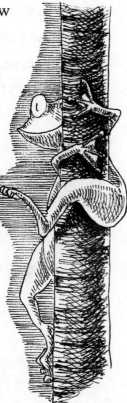

'**Ahhhhhhhh**,' said a voice, and suddenly the Toad found herself being scooped up by something with hot breath and hands that smelled of chocolate.

'Pitty fog,' the voice continued, patting the Toad rather too enthusiastically for her liking.

'Oi!' the Toad croaked. 'Easy does it. I'm not a *dog*.'

Uh-oh, she thought as hot, salty drops began to rain down on her head. Obviously *not* the right thing to say.

'Notta dog. NOTTTTA DoOOOO-OOG,' the voice insisted. 'Wanta my WAYYYYAWOOOo.'

More tears rained down as the Toad tried to slither out of the chocolaty clasp of what appeared to be a stunted red imp. For such a little creature, it possessed a surprisingly tight grip, and try as she might, she couldn't escape.

She wriggled and squirmed, but the red imp clung on. Annoyed, the Toad closed her eyes and tried a very small spell. *Nothing too major*, she thought. *Just a little bolt-from-the-boo spell; a teeny-weeny little electric shock of 10,000 volts or so; enough to make anyone drop whatever they were holding.* Like a toad, for instance.

There was a *flash*, a **crackle** and a . . . nothing. The Toad remained in the embrace of the red imp. This was unheard of. Perhaps the red imp needed to be stung twice before it got the message. The Toad tried again. Still nothing happened. The Toad began to panic.

This red imp was far stronger than she'd imagined. The Toad needed to call for reinforcements. She wriggled round till she could just about make out the lights of home up ahead. Good. That meant the Nose was still awake. Thinking rapidly, she calculated that if only she could persuade this pesky imp to carry her within earshot of the Nose, between herself and her Sister, surely they'd be able to raise enough magical *Vim and Vigour* to force the red imp to let go.

'Um,' she said, 'this, er, *Waywoo* you mentioned?'

WAAAAAYYYYYWOoOooOoOo, Way – my Wayyyy-*hic*-Way-*hic*-WOoOOO?'

'Yes – **arrrgh** – ouch – don't – squee— **Ow**!' the Toad squawked. 'I think I saw your – **Ow** – Waywoo head for that – **Ow** – house up there.'

Immediately the tears and hiccups and squeezes stopped, and in the sudden hush the Toad could hear the sound of the red imp breathing heavily as it gave the Toad's brazen lie its complete attention. After a minute's deep thought, the creature seemed to reach a decision; then, clasping the Toad firmly under her arm, Witch Baby set off for Arkon House to find WayWoof.

As I get closer to Arkon House, I'm really starting to panic. I can't see any sign of Daisy up ahead, and there isn't a sound from the woods where Vivaldi should be. And needless to say, WayWoof hasn't appeared out of the darkness. Not yet, anyway. All I can think of is how horrible it must be for Daisy, out there in the dark, looking for her beloved lost dog, all on her own. Then the thought occurs to me that I'll never be able to go home again if I don't find Daisy. I think it would be easier to live out here in the dark and cold, all on my own, for the rest of my life than go back to Mum and Dad and Jack with the news that Lily the **Bad** Big Sister managed to lose the baby. Help. I can't bear to think about it. Like WayWoof, Daisy simply *has* to turn up. She *must* be up ahead somewhere.

I'm peering into the blackness beyond the gates to Arkon House when I hear footsteps behind me.

'DAISY?'

I spin round, but it's Vivaldi, and she's not holding my little sister's hand. She is alone, and breathing hard as if she's been running.

'No luck?'

'Nope,' Vivaldi says. 'Which means she must be up ahead of us somewhere because she's far too small to have gone any further.'

Vivaldi has a point, but the problem with having a sister who's a **Witch Baby** is that there's no way I can predict what she's going to

do next. For all I know she could be flapping overhead on pterodactyl wings, or burrowing underground like a mole or—

'What's *that*?' Vivaldi hisses in my ear.

Two glowing eyes loom out of the darkness ahead. The split second before I scream my head off and run for my life, Vivaldi's question is answered.

'Hoo – hoooOOOOOO.' And with a beat of its wings, a huge barn owl launches itself off a tree branch and heads for Arkon House. Its graceful flight is slightly hampered by something it is clutching in its claws. Something that wriggles and flails, its legs thrashing in all directions as it tries and fails to escape. I feel slightly sick watching this mid-air struggle. Beautiful as owls are, I can't help feeling sorry for their prey. This victim in particular is putting up one heck of a fight.

Now even the owl appears to be having difficulty hanging onto such a quarrelsome dinner. Lower and lower it flies, its wings dipping first to the right, then to the left, until, finally coming in low over Arkon House's swimming pool, it gives up the battle.

There's a *splash*, and the bird soars back up into the night, its white wings making it look like a ghost. Ripples widen across the leaf-strewn surface of the pool, and on the far side a large frog hoists itself out of the water. The poor

156

creature keeps looking nervously up at the sky, as if it's expecting the owl to return any second now. Shaking itself dry, it leaps into the shadows and disappears. I strain to see where it went, but it is far too dark to make out much beyond the path that winds up to the front door of Arkon House.

'Come on.' Vivaldi has speeded up, as if she can't wait to get this bit over and done with. 'I bet you anything you like that Daisy'll have got there before us.'

There? Arkon House? The thought of poor little Daisy toddling up to that gloomy tomb of a house gives me the CREEPS. Why on earth would anyone *ever* choose to live in a place like that? However, it doesn't look as if there's anyone home tonight, because the entire house is in darkness except for one light in a downstairs window. Welcoming, NOT. We creep towards the lit window, trying not to make any noise, just in case there are burglar alarms or guard dogs or . . .

After her brush with death, the Toad had finally managed to stop shaking and was carefully making her way back home when the white owl struck again. There was a **whoosh**, followed

by a **zipping** sound as a pair of lethally sharp claws whizzed past the Toad's head, missing her by a wart's width.

'**AAAARGH!**' wailed the Toad, dodging behind a tree. 'Leave me alone, you brute!'

'Notta boot,' the white owl said, landing on a branch and peering down at the Toad with its huge eyes. Fluffing its feathers and shaking out its wings, it said proudly, 'Notta boot, silly fog, I'm a howl.'

The Toad's eyes widened. *Wait a minute,* she thought. *I've heard that voice before.* Her brain almost glowed with the effort as she slowly connected talking white owl with red imp, added them together and arrived at—

'**Witch Baby**! Is that . . . can it be, I mean . . . is that *you*?'

The talking white owl blinked, but remained silent.

'It's *me*,' the Toad babbled. 'Me. Your very own loving Toad. *You* know. I'm a witch, just like you.'

'Notta wits,' the talking white owl said, adding, 'Silly fog. I'm a howl.'

The Toad groaned and was just about to point out that she wasn't a frog, she was a toad, and not just any old toad, but a *Toad* toad, when there came the sound of more voices.

'Is that you?' and, 'DAISEEEEEE,' they called, and then came the sound of footsteps. Loud **thudding** footsteps, heading the Toad's way. When you're as small as a toad, the approach of feet is rarely *A Good Thing*. There wasn't enough time to hide, so the Toad pressed her body up against a tree trunk and tried to make herself as SMALL as possible.

The footsteps stopped and the Toad could hear the sound of breathing very close by. She risked a quick look. Large patches of shadow had materialized overhead. Judging by their size, they were children. *Two of them*. The moment they spoke, the Toad recognized them:  Witch Baby's big sister and her friend. The Blue Moon girls.*

'I know she's here. I heard her,' said Witch Baby's sister.

'But there's nobody here,' said her friend. 'Maybe you heard her voice coming from the house?'

'Daisy. Stop playing silly games and come out now.'

There came a mocking 'HOOoo? HOOoOT?' from the treetops; overhead, Daisy spread her wings and glided away, her

* At this, the Toad was barely able to suppress a squeak of terror. Blue Moonies could *see*. Blue Moonies could spot a witch a mile away. If the Blue Moonies got past the front door of Arkon House and spotted the Halloween-enhanced Nose with her whippy hair, eyes of fire and sparky fingertips . . . well, then they'd know *immediately* that she was a witch, and *that* would be the end of the Sisters of Hiss's lovely quiet life. The Blue Moonies would *immediately* tell their parents, their parents would tell their telephones, and before the Sisters of Hiss could throw so much as a brain-wipe or a memory-fog spell, television cameras would be rolling up their front driveway, news-hounds would camp on the lawn and the Sisters of Hiss would never have a moment's peace ever again.

moonshadow falling across the path leading to
Arkon House. A second later, three silhouettes
ran in pursuit of the Daisy-Owl, two girls
running flat out and, some way behind, a large
toad.

Thirteen:

A little bit of bat

At first the Nose thought someone was playing a trick on her. Hair thrashing wildly, fingertips fizzing and magic fairly pouring out of her ears, she had almost *flown* across the hall to answer the door. To her huge disappointment, there was nobody there. Then she looked down and saw the white owl. She was just wondering why there was an owl on her doorstep when she saw the two bandaged figures racing towards her.

'Daisy!' one of them yelled, and the Nose immediately realized who the figures were. With a **hiss**, she slammed the door shut and turned the key in the lock. In her haste to shut it, she completely failed to recognize the true identity of the owl standing on her doorstep.

There. Now those awful Blue Moon girls

could bang and knock on the door till the moon turned into green gorgonzola, but the Nose would *never* let them in. Never. **Eeughhhh**. She **shuddered**. Blue Moon girls were almost worse than Witch Babies That Didn't Go According to Plan.*

Blue Moon girls were the bane of a witch's life. Blue Moon girls were nosy, clever, talkative, and in clusters of more than one, downright dangerous. One Blue Moon girl might say, *Oooh, look, there's a witch*, but nobody would believe her. But *two* Blue Moon girls? They would back each other up. They would say, *WE saw a witch*. People would pay attention to two

---

* Just before Daisy was born, the Sisters of Hiss had cooked up a brilliant plan to turn a human baby into a Witch Baby. Their plan involved magic, full moons, warts, tonsils, memory and a great deal of meaningless muttering. They'd even found the perfect baby girl for turning into a Witch Baby: the newborn Daisy MacRae, who, all unknowing, lay gurgling happily in an Edinburgh maternity hospital while the Sisters of Hiss put their plan into action.
However, at some point during the meaningless-muttering part of the spell, one or two — or perhaps all three — Sisters made a small, but ultimately disastrous Spelling Mistake. And as any witch can tell you, once made, a Spelling Mistake *cannot be undone*. Hence Daisy, the Witch Baby Who Does Exactly As She Pleases.

of the gabby little pests. Two Blue Moon girls meant *trouble*.

The Nose was about to explode with bottled-up **Halloween** magic. It took several repetitions of the **Wheesht spell*** to stop her from sending a bolt of lightning after the Blue Moon girls. By the time she'd finally managed to calm down, not only was the Nose exhausted, she was also *ravenous*. She staggered into the kitchen, helped herself to the contents of the fridge, raided the Toad's hidden stash of chocolate, and with a box of special foil-wrapped chocolate mints under one arm, headed for the living room, where she turned the TV on to its loudest volume and collapsed into a sofa.

Which explained why she didn't hear the Toad's increasingly desperate pleas to open the

---

* *Wheesht* is Old Caledonian for *shutte uppe*. Here's the spell to stop uncontrollable eruptions of magic:

> Tether, truss, lash and bind,
> Keep your Magick tightly twined,
> Padlock, latch, bolt and chain,
> Keep your spells locked in your brain.

door and let her back inside. Even though the Toad knew that it was really dear little Witch Baby underneath that beak and those claws, the way the white owl kept staring at her was making her feel very nervous indeed.

'Let me *in*,' she yelled. 'Open the blooming door, would you?' But every window and door appeared to have been shut, locked and bolted against her. Jumping up and down outside the living-room window, the Toad could see the Nose sprawled across the sofa, lit by the flickering glow from the TV.

'HELP!' she shrieked, sliding back down the window in between each despairing attempt to gain her Sister's attention. 'HELP MEEEE! LET MEEEE IN!'

To the Toad's fury, not only was the Nose deaf to her cries, but she appeared to be shovelling handfuls of gold foil-wrapped chocolates down

her throat. The Toad's eyes widened. *Wait a minute . . .* she thought. *Those sweets are* mine. *Those sweets are from my secret stash of foil-wrapped chocolate mints.*

That was the final straw. A mist rose before the Toad's eyes and murderous thoughts filled her mind. She turned bright flame-red and grew a metre in all directions. Turning to face the white owl, she opened her mouth and long ribbons of fire poured out.

Daisy's owl-eyes widened. Something had gone horribly wrong with her funny frog-toy.

'GO WAY. No like it, FOG,' she said, and with a flurry of feathers she took off, more like a rocket than an owl. Seconds later, there was a smash, a shriek and a crash as a television flew across the garden. This was promptly followed by a pitter-pattering sound as a box of foil-wrapped chocolate mints followed in the wake of the TV.

The Toad was home.

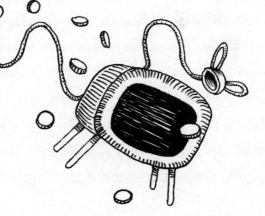

We're running after the Daisy-Owl, begging her to slow down. It's all very well flying through the dark if you've got wings, but keeping up on foot is almost impossible.

'OW!' yells Vivaldi, stumbling on tree roots.

'OUCH!' I shriek, falling into a ditch.

'HOOO-HOOO,' calls my little sister, fluttering up ahead.

I have no idea why Daisy took off like a rocket from round the side of Arkon House. The big-nosed lady who answered the door and then slammed it shut in our faces looked very much like the old lady with cheese in her hair who Jack and I had seen in the woods the day before. But whoever she was, she obviously didn't feel like handing out any Halloween treats. No matter how many times we knocked on the door, she ignored us. By then, all we wanted to do was reassure ourselves that WayWoof wasn't inside, then get as far away from Arkon House as possible. Since the front door remained firmly shut, Vivaldi and I decided to sniff our way round the outside of the house trying to catch a whiff of WayWoof.

As Vivaldi said, 'We have to *think* like a dog in order to have any chance of finding her,' and to prove her point, my mad friend got down on all fours and pretended to scratch behind her ear with one leg. I let my tongue loll out of the side of my mouth and rolled on my back with

all four paws – I mean, my arms and legs – in the air. But fun as this was, it wasn't really helping with finding WayWoof. We sniffed harder, but we couldn't detect so much as an atom of *Pong de Pooch*. We tried by the bins (**eughhh**), the drains (**Poooo**), and even started digging in a flowerbed like WayWoof would.* Try as we might to take ourselves seriously, we kept on bursting into nervous giggles.

Sniff, sniff, **snorrrrrrt**.

'Why don't mummies take holidays?' Vivaldi whispered.

I had no idea, so I kept on sniffing.

'Because . . .' Vivaldi could barely get the words out, she was so giggly. 'Because they're afraid to relax and unwind!' She collapsed in a heap in the flowerbed at the same time as Daisy took off like an express train.

---

* While this didn't help us find WayWoof, our dig through the flowerbed turned up six foil-wrapped chocolate mint coins. Being noble mummies, Vivaldi and I didn't eat these, but added them to the Halloween loot.

And now we're running **madly** through the woods, bounding pell-mell downhill. We're following Daisy, who is flying like an expert considering what a beginner owl she is. She swoops and glides over the treetops, **hooting**

with delight, effortlessly riding the wind. By comparison, Vivaldi and I are stumbling around like a pair of hippos and panting like steam engines as we try to catch up with my little sister.

'Waaaaait up,' Vivaldi yells. 'We can't keep up with youuuuuu · · ·' But her voice is swept away by the wind and Daisy flies on, giving no sign of having heard. Poor Vivaldi – she's an amateur when it comes to dealing with Witch Babies, whereas I've been on the receiving end of Daisy's particular kind of baby magic for a year and a half. I'm pretty sure I know how to get my sister to pay attention.

'OI, SQUIRT!' I bawl, hands on either side of my mouth to make myself into **LILY THE HUMAN FOGHORN**.* 'WE'VE GOT ALL THE **Halloween** SWEETS, NOT YOU-HOOO.' I'm one hundred per cent certain that the owl's wing beats have slowed down, but she hasn't turned round yet, the baggage. *Hmmmm.* Time to pile on the pressure. 'OOOH, *MY*, THESE ARE GOING TO BE *SOOOOO* GOOD. I'M UNWRAPPING A CHOCOLATE TRUFFLE RIGHT NowwWAAARGH.' And suddenly I've got a face full of outraged owl.

* Mum passed this ability on to me in her genes. We MacRae women have lungs like . . . well, like bagpipes actually. If we wanted to, we could shatter windows in buildings a mile away with just one shriek.

See? Daisy may be a **Witch Baby**, but she'll always be the Squirt to me.

To fortify ourselves before we head for Yoshito's, we each eat one of Annabel's chocolate champagne truffles. They're *amazing*. Unfortunately Daisy dribbles some of hers down her front, so her feathers turn a revolting shade of brown, despite my efforts to wipe them clean with a handful of leaves.

'Toppit, Lil.' Daisy pushes me away with her beak.

'Um . . . Daze,' I begin. 'What about changing into something else before we get to Yoshito's?'

Daisy ignores me and turns her attention to grooming under her wings.

'Uhhh, how about something a wee bit less realistic?' I'm worried that Yoshito or her dad will be so impressed by Daisy's costume that, just like Vivaldi's mum, they'll try to work out how it's made. 'What about changing into a **WITCH**?'

'No wantit wits,' Daisy says with such scorn that I blush. How stupid am I? Daisy *is* a witch. She doesn't have to dress like one to prove it.

Vivaldi comes to my rescue. 'Or . . . um . . . how about a vampire? Or, *I* know – what about a *werewolf*?'

Oh, no. **OH, NO**. Oh, for heaven's sake. Vivaldi's hands fly up to her mouth as if to try and stifle what she just said; to cram it back down her throat again before Daisy can hear. But it's too late.

WAYYYYYYYYYYYWOooo-Ooooooo – wanta my WAYWOOo – *hic*

-WAY- *hic* -WOoOºo.'

Oh, dear. Daisy calms down eventually, but it takes the remaining three chocolate champagne truffles to finally stop her tears. By the time she's smeared truffle-dribble down her front, across her feathers and all round her beak, you can't tell *what* she is supposed to be. Then, just as we arrive at **Yoshito's** round house, Daisy finally decides it's time to change into something different. Gone are the chocolate feathers, and in their place is an exceedingly hairy version of that old **Halloween** favourite, the **VAMPIRE**. At least, I *think* that's what she is – except from where I'm standing I can see that her feet are hovering a few inches *above* Yoshito's doorstep, which means . . . she's probably a *bat*, not a vampire after all.

Which is fine, just as long as she doesn't start to fly—

'Lily! Vivaldi! Oh, and little Daisy too – come in, come in.' The door opens and there is a *dragon* welcoming us into the house.

'Not a dragon, Lily,' Yoshito whispers, closing the door behind us. 'I'm a koi carp.'

Whatever she is, she looks *incredible*. She glows and glitters, with diamonds of light sparkling off thousands of spangles and sequins sewn the length of her costume. Her headdress is covered in tiny mirrors, so when I look at her

I can only see her eyes surrounded by millions of tiny chopped-up reflections of myself. Oh, dear. I'd forgotten that I am Lily, the maggot. This has got to be the worst thing I've ever worn at **Halloween**. Now that I'm inside Yoshito's house I can see that my costume is already falling apart. My pink bandages are coming undone and leaving shreds of pink thread everywhere I walk. Mind you, Vivaldi is unravelling too and she looks great. Perhaps it's not such a disaster after all. After two or three thousand years, even the best-dressed mummies would be beginning to look a little the worse for wear.

Yoshito waves a hand at a spiral staircase in the middle of her hall. 'Papa and I are upstairs. Do you like our lanterns?'

WOW. What an *amazing* house. There are enormous paper lanterns shining all the way up the stairs. They're hanging on the thinnest

threads so that they look as if they're floating in space. Guided by Yoshito, we begin to climb, and to my amusement I notice that Daisy is so overawed by this house that she's not floating or flapping like a **bat** any more. She's *hopping* upstairs, thank heavens.

The stairs wind up in a seemingly never-ending spiral of glass steps. It makes me feel dizzy being able to see all the way down *through* them to the hall below. From somewhere up above we can hear the murmur of voices and the faint sound of music.

'Have you had other guisers visiting tonight?' Vivaldi asks.

'Yes,' Yoshito says. 'Papa has a friend round who is disguising as a witch.' She drops her voice to a whisper and adds, 'Her disguising isn't very good. Nothing like as brilliant as you and Vivaldi.'

'Me too. Lookit *me*,' Daisy says, determined not to be upstaged by a pair of mere mummies, especially when one of them is wrapped in unravelling pink strips and looks like a shredded worm.

Yoshito smiles, but doesn't say anything. Daisy frowns. Obviously she was hoping for more, so she flaps her wings to encourage Yoshito to say something in praise of her vampire-or-possibly-bat disguise.

Ah. She's definitely a *bat*. How do I know this? Oh, sigh. Daisy has flipped herself upside down and is dangling from the ceiling above the stairs, yelling, 'LOOKIT *meeeeeee*, WHEEEEEEE, lookit *me*.'

Oh, dear. Can we go now? Before she does something worse – like raining bat-poo down on our heads or turning into a **VAMPIRE** bat and *biting* someone? How on earth am I supposed to explain this to Yoshito? As if my costume wasn't embarrassing enough, now Daisy is behaving like a complete **WITCH**. I turn to Yoshito to try to make some excuse, and all my words dry up and wither in my mouth.

Oh, NO.

I look at Vivaldi.

Oh, triple NO with knobs on.

Oh, AAAAARGH.

Oh, Daisy, what have you *done*?

Fourteen:

The Chin chills out

To her surprise, the Chin was having a wonderful time being fussed over by Mr Harukashi and his daughter. From the moment the child had introduced herself from the back seat of the car as they sped away from Arkon House, the Chin had been stunned. She'd had no idea that human children were so *inquisitive*. Within seconds of meeting the Chin, Yoshito Harukashi had locked eyes with her in the car's

rear-view mirror, and begun the Inquisition. Did she like fish? Which fish was her favourite? Did she like swimming? Pool, river or sea? What was her favourite colour? Season? Word? Food? Book? Animal? And without pausing once for breath, the tiny eight-year-old girl began to worm her way into the heavily guarded fortress of the Chin's affections.

Being grilled nonstop for answers made the Chin feel as if she'd been turned into a piece of furniture; like a chest of drawers through which someone was having a good rummage, hunting for a stray sock. It wasn't in the least unpleasant, but the Chin realized that she had to be very careful not to give away anything too important. Like the fact she was a **WITCH**, for instance . . . So not a whisper about magic, broomstick or spells. Not so much as a squeak about **Witch Baby**. Fixing a pleasant smile across her face, the Chin tried her best to stay afloat in the flood of questions. Finally, when she was sure that Yoshito had asked her every possible question, and some impossible ones as well, Hare slowed down and swung the car into the driveway of his house. He leaped out and came round to open the door for his guest of honour.

In the few seconds when the Chin and Yoshito were alone, the little girl said urgently, 'Excuse me, Miss Chin, for asking so many questions, but I must find out who you really are.'

The Chin's eyes widened. *What?* In a panic, she began to scrabble at the catch on her seatbelt, but Yoshito continued, 'I only wish for my papa to be happy. He thinks that you are a sweet and kind old lady, but you and I, well – we know differently, don't we?'

'Pardon?' the Chin gasped, inwardly thinking, *HELP. The child knows I'm a witch. Mayday, mayday,* AOOOOGARGH, while managing to squeak, 'Whatever do you take me for?'

Yoshito smiled happily and clapped her hands. 'Oh, Miss Chin, you don't have to pretend with me. I think you're our *fairy godmother*!'

The Chin blinked rapidly. What on *earth*? Before she could reply, Hare Harukashi opened the passenger door and helped her clamber out.

'I think my little Yoshi has really taken to you, Miss Chin.'

Are you kidding? the Chin thought. *Your daughter just ate me alive. If I survive the evening, it'll be a miracle worthy of a fairy godmother.*

Hare Harukashi was beaming at the Chin, obviously delighted with how well the evening was progressing. 'Come, my dear Miss Chin, welcome to our little home.' And proudly, Hare ushered his guest inside.

Hare turned out to be not only a wonderful host but an excellent cook as well. After a delicious supper of fish cunningly carved into rectangles and covered with tiny orange crumbs ('Delighted you like them, Miss Chin. Fish fingers are Yoshi's favourite') and potatoes he'd cleverly transformed into golden, crisp batons

('I cannot believe you have never eaten a chip before, dear lady'), the Chin settled back into a comfy chair and sipped at a cup of tea. She could hardly remember an evening that she'd enjoyed as much as this. Despite Yoshito's endless questions, she was so relaxed that she felt as if she were about to melt into a little puddle of contentment. All she'd had to do was be pleasant; in return, the Harukashis had treated her as if she were the funniest, cleverest, most beautiful and precious person ever to walk the earth. *If this was what being a fairy godmother was all about*, the Chin thought sleepily, *then perhaps it was time for a career change*. She was happily daydreaming about her new, improved self: the frothy petticoats, the sparkly tiaras, the gossamer wings— When abruptly the dream came to an end.

The
doorbell rang,
and excusing
herself, Yoshito
ran downstairs to
answer it.

'Ah, that will be
Yoshi's guests,' Mr Harukashi
said, refilling the Chin's cup with tea.

'Children?' she asked, her voice emerging as a hoarse squawk. If she had her way as a *fairy godmother*, she'd turn all the children in Scotland except Yoshito into pumpkins.

'From the school,' Hare explained, adding, 'Lovely children. Lily and Vivaldi. Yoshi talks about them all the time . . .'

Inside the Chin's brain, alarm bells were sounding. *Lily* and *Vivaldi*? The Blue Moon girls? This was **bad**. This was very, very **bad** indeed. In fact, this was a complete **disaster**.

What to do? If the Blue Moon girls saw her, especially tonight, with all that extra **Halloween magic** around, they might recognize that she was a **WITCH**; then they might find out where she lived and *that* would be the end of the **Sisters of HiSS** living in peace at Arkon House. The Chin's eyes swivelled from side to side as she tried to think how she could avoid being found out. She could throw a memory-fog spell, but when you're trying to disguise the fact that you're a witch, throwing spells at **Halloween** was a **Very Bad Idea**. **Halloween** tended to magnify the effect if you didn't pay attention to what you were doing. Besides, the Chin realized that she'd forgotten the exact words of the memory-fog spell. Was it a *ram* or a *rom* after the *tiddly-pom*?

She **groaned** out loud. What to do? She could simply vanish, but she suspected that Hare and Yoshito would be terribly upset, and might even come looking for her, all the way back to Arkon House – and who knew what mischief the Nose and the Toad might have got up to in her absence? The Chin **shuddered**. All of a sudden she wanted to go home. Just to check that everything was all right. To make sure that her Sisters weren't hurling the best china at each other . . .

Talking of which . . . suddenly the Chin had an idea. Not the *best* idea she'd ever had, but it would have to do. She reached for her teacup, and waiting till Mr Harukashi's attention was elsewhere, she deliberately dropped it in her lap.

'AAAAarrrrggghhHHHH!'

she yelled; then, for good measure, 'OoOoyeeeoWwWwOuCh!' And to make sure that Mr Harukashi got the message, she stood up, slipped on the wet floor, skidded across the living room and fell into the log basket with a despairing *wail*.

There. That ought to do it.

Fifteen:

The pesky bat mobile

If you've ever wondered what it would be like to have wings, I can tell you. It feels like *wwwwwwwwwwwwwwwwwwwwwwwwwwwwwwwwwwwwwwwwwhhheeeeeeee*. No sooner had I discovered that I was mysteriously covered in silky black fur and attached to a huge leathery cape than I
began   falling

back$_w$a$_r$d$_s$

$\quad$ d

$\quad\quad$ o

$\quad\quad\quad$ w

$\quad\quad\quad\quad$ n

Yoshito's stairs.

I put my hands out to save myself and . . . yyyyyyeeeeeeeeeee-eeeeeeeeeeeeaaaaaa-aaaooooOWWWW!

I took off. WOW. WOW. How amazing is that? I've dreamed about being able to do this, but *really* flying is absolutely the best thing ever. With one effortless flap I soar up to the ceiling and circle round; then I take a deep breath, and holding my leathery wings close to my body, I dive down, faster and faster and faster till my eyes are streaming and everything is a blur; and then, at the last second, I unfurl my wings and swoop up, up, up again. Oh,

YESSSSSSS. This is the best magic spell Daisy has *ever* done.

Fluttering and flapping around me are Daisy, Vivaldi and Yoshito; all *four* of us now turned into **bats**, thanks to my little sister and her witchy ways. Trust me, when people say that their wee sisters are driving them batty, they have no *idea* what they're talking about. I hope Vivaldi and Yoshito aren't too freaked out by what Daisy has done to them, but judging by the loop-the-loops and mid-air somersaults they're doing, they can't be too upset. After a while we all fly up to one of the lanterns and hang upside down from it to catch our breath.

Being a **bat** is *brilliant*. I'm just about to launch myself into the air again when I see Yoshito madly flapping to get my attention. What? What's wrong? Yoshito points with a wing to where, far below, her dad is ushering an old lady

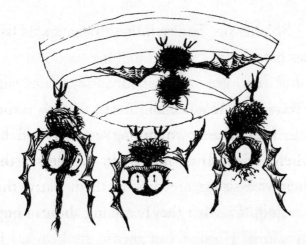

into the bathroom. The door closes behind her and Mr Harukashi returns to the living room.

Fortunately he didn't look up and see us. We're all clinging to a lantern and trying to make ourselves as invisible as possible. This is because not everyone welcomes free-range bats in their houses, even for **Halloween**. Time to go, I think. Time to continue the search for **WayWoof**. I edge closer to Daisy and flap to get her attention.

'Come on, Squirt. Time to change us back so that we can carry on looking for . . . um . . . carry on our search for . . . er . . . to find *Things We Might Have Lost*.'* This is what I meant to say, but what came out was a series of high-pitched squeaks: 'Eeeek – – eee – ee-ee-eeEEEEe-e-e-e-e.'

Help. This isn't *fair*. Daisy-as-a-bat can speak in normal Human, but apparently I can't. I try again.

'Come *on*, Daze. Not funny. Change us back, eh? We've got things to do, houses to check, er . . . chocolate to earn?'

It's no good. I'm *squeaking*, not speaking.

Daisy, the baggage, peers at me and says, 'Not lissnin', Lil. What say? *Eee? Eeeeh?*' And she dissolves into giggles before flapping off downstairs and back up again, which is like a bat going **Nya-nya-nee-nyaa-na**.

---

* Clever, eh? Notice that I didn't mention WayWoof by name.

Aaaaaargh. Did I mention how stubborn Daisy can be? At this rate we could be stuck here all night until my **WITCH** of a sister decides she's had enough of this spell.

Then, just when I think it can't get any worse, from somewhere deep in Vivaldi's fur, an alarm begins to ring. With a dismayed squeak she plucks something out from under her wing. It's her mobile phone, shrunk to the right size for a bat to use, should a bat wish to make phone calls. However, mobile keypads aren't designed for bats, and no matter what Vivaldi does, she

can't make the alarm shut up. To our horror, it's one of those alarms that grows louder and louder, the longer they're left to ring. AAaARRRGH. It now sounds like a fire alarm, but even though all three of us poke and slap and even *bite* the phone, we aren't able to silence the din. We flutter down to land on one of the glass stair treads and take turns jumping up and down on the keypad, but still the phone keeps ringing. This is rapidly turning into a total **NIGHTMARE**. If we don't find a way to turn it off, Yoshito's dad is going to come out of the living room to find out what on earth is going on. I feel like I'm in the middle of a very bad dream* that will end with Yoshito's dad discovering that not only has he got four *bats*

* One of those awful ones where you're being chased by the
slavering, terrifying Beast of Boggart Moor and you're running
flat out, gasping for breath, stumbling though deep puddles,
wading through sticky swamps with brambles and thorns ripping
at your legs, and you turn to check that the B of BM isn't
gaining on you. It is. And as it turns its awful stare upon
you . . . you're paralysed. Unable to move a muscle. Well and
truly stuck. Standing there, frozen, with your mouth open for
all time in an awful silent scream . . . because you are about
to become breakfast, lunch and dinner for the B of BM, which
will shudder to a stop in front of you, its wide slobbery mouth
open in a grin of sheer delight, its ragged claws reaching out
to— I'll leave the rest to your imagination.

in his house, but they've brought their own shriek-alarm.

Fortunately, while I've been unable to think of a single thing to save us, Vivaldi's brain has been working overtime. She takes her mobile, holds it out over the central stairwell, then deliberately drops it down all three flights, shrieking all the way (the phone, that is, *not* Vivaldi).

There's a tiny crash . . . then blissful silence. I'm so impressed, I start clapping, which is when I realize I have *hands*, not wings. So do Daisy, Yoshito and Vivaldi. Spell over.

Then Daisy says, 'All gone. Poo phone. All boken.'

And it is. We run down to the bottom of the stairs to check, but the phone is in pieces. Vivaldi heaves a sigh as we help her gather up the bits, but then she manages to smile.

'It was worth it. I *loved* being a bat.'

Yoshito looks bemused. 'Did I just dream that I was flying?' She rubs her eyes and stretches out her arms as wide as they can go. 'So . . . weird. When we were running up and down-stairs, I almost felt as if I had wings . . . as if I was a **bat** . . .'

I **freeze**. What can I say? *Well, yes. You* did *have wings. Actually, Yoshito, you* were *turned into a bat by my little sister who, you may be surprised to learn, is a witch?* No. I don't *think* so. I stare at Vivaldi, willing her to say something – anything – to change the subject, but for once Vivaldi seems to have run out of words. In the end it's Daisy who bridges the awkward silence.

'Dunna poo, Lil-Lil,' she mutters, then adds with unnecessary relish, 'Wipe my bum-bum.'

AAAAaRrRrGH. Time to go home. Time to hand my little sister back to her ever-loving, bottom-laundering parents. Time to hit the road.

It isn't until the three of us are back outside in the darkness, our bag of **Halloween** loot enlarged by the addition of three fish-shaped chocolate bars and a box of After Eights, that Daisy demonstrates how terrifically *useful* magic can be.

'Lookit, Lil-Lil,' she says, digging her hands under the waistband of her nappy. 'Notta poo now.'

I take several rapid steps backwards, just in case she's wrong, or I misheard her, or—

Daisy is pulling handfuls of white fluff from her nappy. Heaps and heaps of it, as if she were a soft toy with its stuffing coming out. How

weird is this? And what on earth—

'Not dunna poo, Lil-Lil,' Daisy squeals, obviously delighted at her own wit. 'Dunna woo. Woo, woo. *Baa baa back seep, havva bitta* WOOOOOOOO,' and then she laughs so hard she has to sit down.

Oh, sigh. Still, better a woo than a **poo**, any day.

Oh, *double* sigh. I cannot believe I just thought that.

Sixteen:

The fairly oddmother

The Chin waited until she was sure that Mr Harukashi had returned to the living room before she dared open the bathroom door as much as a whisker's width. When the small bat fluttered past her line of vision, she shut the door at once. Being a witch herself, she immediately realized that the bat was a magically altered girl; and not just *any* girl, but a *Blue Moon* one. **Hissing** furiously to herself, she considered her options.

Escape via the door was now out of the question, thanks to those pestilential Blue Moon brats. Turning in a circle, the Chin saw that she couldn't have chosen a worse room from which to plan her escape. The bathroom was tiny, and in place of where a window should be, there was

only an extractor fan. Inwardly cursing the penny-pinching builder who had built this windowless witch-trap, the Chin sat on the toilet to work out what on earth to do next. Obviously she couldn't remain in the bathroom for too much longer or Mr Harukashi would smell a rat . . .

A *rat*. That was it! *Perfect*. *And*, with a bit of clever tweaking, both Yoshito and her father would be charmed. Moments later, the Chin was ready. She'd written a thank-you letter on the bathroom mirror with soap:

Dear Hare and Yoshito
Like Cinderella, I must fly.
Thank you both for an
enchanted evening.
Your very own
Fairy Oddmother
Mischin

and placed one of her shoes in the sink underneath. Hoping that she'd remembered the spell correctly,* the Chin closed her eyes and took a deep breath.

Two seconds later, a small brown rat scuttled across the bathroom floor, vaulted onto the toilet seat, clasped its front paws together and performed a perfect swan-dive straight down the U-bend.

* She had. Here it is, minus the hard-to-pronounce bit in Ancient Babbleonian:

```
mus, i, mus          a hisster
her, me, mus         a twister
ver, min, us         chin to grin; grin to grit
verminus             grit to rit; rit to rat
a whisker            That's that.
a sister
```

'Thank heavens Yoshito didn't ask any more questions about wings, bats or whatever,' Vivaldi said as we crossed the Harukashis' garden. 'I have no *idea* how we got away with Daisy turning all of us into bats.'

Phew. That was the closest Daisy has ever come to blowing her cover. The scary thing is that she couldn't care less who finds out that she can do magic. She is quite happy to let the whole *world* know that she's a **WITCH**. I look at her, but she's not paying any attention to Vivaldi and me, because she's fascinated by the Harukashis' fish-shaped pool, which is flickering with tiny flames. As we draw closer, we can see that the flames belong to

hundreds of tea-lights: little candles set on small flower-shaped rafts which float in a pool of darkness.

'**Ahhhhh**,' Daisy says, her eyes growing wide, and then, with no warning, she changes into a lit pumpkin lantern.

I have to point out what a smart move *this* is. Now we have to carry her. All the way round the last few houses and then back home. Oh, sigh.

She turns out not to be too heavy, and she's thoughtfully included her hairband as a kind of lantern handle, so Vivaldi and I take turns carrying her. Daisy glows merrily in our arms, lighting our way through the woods and across a boggy field which Vivaldi assures me is a brilliant short cut to the next houses.

It is neither brilliant nor short. It's wet, cold and full of deep boggy bits. Even with the feeble light from Daisy the Pumpkin, it's too dark to see where I'm putting my feet. Somebody way off in the distance is letting off fireworks, as if they can't wait for Guy Fawkes in five days' time. Every so often there's a huge **KABOOOM** and the night sky is lit by a dazzling flash of light.

Vivaldi splashes on ahead, making enthusiastic noises to encourage me to keep going. 'This is GREAT!' she lies. 'Every time I

come here, I imagine a huge dinosaur is going
to loom out of the mist or a m@nster rise up
out of the bog or . . .'

Thanks, Vivaldi, for that happy thought.
I'm now walking a lot faster to avoid being a
late-night snack for the Beast of the Boggy Short
Cut.

KABOOOM!

Squish, squelch, schloop, I go,
slithering and staggering through thick mud

and over tussocks which I can only see when there's a flash from the fireworks.

KABOOOM!

Squish, squelch, schloop.

'Is it much further?' I wail as I sink up to my knees in cold mud. YEEEURCHHH.

Vivaldi doesn't answer, just plods on determinedly, and I have no choice but to follow, Daisy growing heavier with each footstep.

KABOOOM.

Squish, squelch, schloop.

This is No Fun At All. In fact, I decide, this is The Pits. Then, when I'm sure it can't get any worse, it begins to rain.

'VIVALDEEEEEEEE?' I can just about see her, wading through bogs up ahead. 'I think we're lost.'

Ominously, Vivaldi doesn't deny this. Instead, she stops and waits for me. I **stagger** and **squelch** across to her and put Daisy the Pumpkin down to give my arms a rest. Daisy gives a **hiss** and her light goes out. Oh, *great*. That's all we need. Now I can't see a thing, including where I just dumped Daisy.

'Daisy?'

Silence.

'DAISEEE?'

KABOOOM!

'Lil?' That's Vivaldi calling.

'I've lost the pumpkin lantern!' I wail.

'Don't panic,' Vivaldi calls back. 'Hang on. I'll come over to where you are.'

Squelch, splash, splott.

'Vivaldi? Is that you? There?'

'No. I'm over here, Lil.'

Sploosh. Squerch, schlopp.

Fun as it was watching Lily and Vivaldi wading in circles around each other, Daisy was growing bored with being an extinguished pumpkin lantern. However, thanks to Vivaldi, she had a brilliant idea for what to turn herself into next. As the distant flashes and KABOOMs built up to a dazzling crescendo, and Lily and Vivaldi flailed around in the darkness, unable to find each other, Daisy the dinosaur lumbered away to watch the fireworks.

Seventeen:

Spell it out

The **Sisters of HiSS** were too engrossed in fighting each other to notice the giant shadow of a dinosaur that fell over their swimming pool. The Chin had escaped from the Harukashis, only to find that Arkon House had been turned into a battlefield in her absence. Despite her strict instructions to avoid using magic at **Halloween**, it was obvious that both the Nose and the Toad had been hurling hexes at each other for hours. Caught in a stinging hail of curses, the Chin had no option but to roll up her sleeves and join in.

KABOOOM went the Chin's Marshmallow Mortar spell, making

the ground shake as it covered the Toad and the Nose in a monsoon of sticky white goo. Coughing as she picked marshmallow out of her vast nostrils, the Nose flexed her fingers, racked her brains for the right words, and then, with a huge **FLASH**HHHHH, replied with a Fossicking Furball, which carpeted everything around it in black fur.

The combination of being slathered in marshmallow and then dusted with fur so infuriated the Toad that instead of attempting to make peace between her Sisters, she threw a Soup-pot spell. All at once it began to rain minestrone, and gigantic soup-pots of every shape and colour began to gather

like thunderheads in the sky above
Arkon House.

In the middle of a particularly heavy
pea-and-pasta squall, Daisy the Dinosaur
stepped out from behind a tree and loudly
demanded, 'What doon, witses?'

The spectacle of all **Daisy's** rows of dinosaur
teeth glinting in the darkness made the
Sisters of Hiss pause in mid-battle. In fact,
for one moment they were so paralysed with
fear that they failed to recognize who was
looming over them with her claws
outstretched in such a terrifying manner. Then
the Toad spotted a familiar headband wrapped

round one of the dinosaur's horns, and all
became clear.

'Don't panic, dear Sisters!' she yelled. 'It's only our own precious Witch Baby.'

'Witch B-B-B-Baby?' the Chin quavered. 'How on earth did she ever get to be that size?'

'Pffffff,' the Nose snorted. '*Anyone* can turn themselves into a dinosaur at Halloween. Dinosaurs are easy-peasy.' To prove how unimpressed she was with Daisy's spells, she marched up to the dinosaur and poked at its rear end. 'I mean, look at this tail. It's the wrong *colour*. They're meant to be *green*, not pink. I could do better with my eyes shut.'

'No likeit, wits,' the dinosaur muttered, a loud **rumbling** sound coming from its middle.

'What was that?' the Nose whispered nervously. 'That sort of thundering sound?'

'**Need a nutha POO**,' the dinosaur roared miserably, turning round to peer in reproach at its tail. 'Need a—'

And before the Sisters of Hiss could take cover or throw another spell to protect themselves, there came a thundering roar, followed by a **choking** cloud of noxious gas, and then the dinosaur erupted.

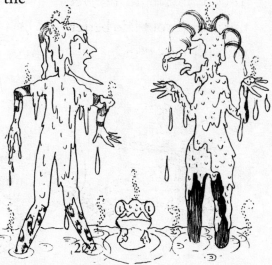

At which point, aware that she'd probably done **A Bad Thing**, Daisy the Dinosaur vanished into the night.

This is the worst night of my entire life. After what feels like *hours* of wallowing around in cold mud, yelling each other's names, hugging trees and falling into keep boggy bits, Vivaldi and I finally find each other. However,

it's beginning to look like I've managed to lose Daisy (again). And to make matters worse, it's pitch dark, we're up to our knees in mud and it's raining hard. Oh yes, and *we still haven't found WayWoof.*

Suddenly I'm so sick of **Halloween** that all I want to do is scream. At this rate we're *never* going to find WayWoof. We don't know why she vanished, and we haven't a clue where she's gone. Didn't she like us any more? Right up until she vanished, I was so sure she loved us as much as we loved her. **Oh**, **WayWoof** – if only we knew why you'd gone, we'd have a better idea of *where* you might be. All I can think of is that she must have gone somewhere quiet to have her babies. Like humans do. When Mum and Dad went to have Daisy at the hospit—

It's as if a light has switched on behind my eyes. Suddenly I know why WayWoof has run away, and I have a good idea where she has gone. It's so ridiculously obvious, I'm amazed it's taken me so long to work it out.

'I'm *nearly* one hundred per cent positive

that she ran away to be with the father of her puppies,' I say, thinking out loud.

'*Who* ran away to be with the father of her pup—? Oh, you mean Way—'

But before Vivaldi can finish what she's saying, two things happen at once. There's a faint shrieking, hissing cry from the direction of where the fireworks were, and then, much closer at hand, we hear something go:

AWOoOoO.

AOWWWWLLLLL. YOWwww11.

What was *that*?

AWooOoOOWWWWLLL.

YowWWWWLLLLLL, it goes again.

Vivaldi grabs my arm. 'That's *her*,' she says. 'I'd recognize that howl anywhere.'

It's an impressive howl. Almost as loud as my bagpipes, and they're *loud*.

'How d'you know it's WayWoof?' The words

are just out of my mouth when I realize that saying WayWoof's name out loud is the best way to find Daisy.

Vivaldi is so excited that she practically foams at the mouth. 'WAYWOOF!' she shrieks. 'It's **WayWoof** – I'd know that howl anywh— Aw, *heck*.'

A mere step or two way, the Pumpkin suddenly blazes fiercely, relighting herself in a blast of yellow fire, and lets rip with a banshee shriek: 'WAAAAAAAAAAAAYYYYy-WOooooOOooOoOo.'

'Um. Sorry, you guys.' Vivaldi closes her eyes and shakes her head. 'I am such a complete and utterly, totally hopeless *numpty*.'

Daisy stops in mid-shriek and her pumpkin eyes swivel* in Vivaldi's direction. Her mouth curves up in a pumpkinny leer and she says, 'Sucha numpy. *NUMPY DUMPY, sittona POOOOOOO.*'**

'Er, yes,' Vivaldi says. 'Well, not exactl—'

'*Sucha NUMPY sattona POOOOOOOO.*'

Oh, dear – but at least we've found the Pumpkin, and she isn't crying any more and we're getting closer to the source of the Howl. AWOOOOOHOWWWWLLLLL.

Now that we're heading in the right direction, I'm feeling more and more certain that this is where WayWoof will be. We can see

---

* Yup. This is every bit as weird as it sounds. Especially since we can see that there's nothing *inside* Daisy's head except three lit candle stubs. I hope she changes back into herself before Mum and Dad catch sight of Daisy the Illuminated Squash-with-no-brain.

** My little sister loves poo jokes. Any possible place where she can drop in a poo or two, she'll do it. Er. That's *not* what I mean.

where we're going now, because the rain has stopped and the moon has slid out from behind the clouds. As we get nearer, we realize that the distant howling is mingled with the chorus of many cat voices, all of them impatiently demanding their supper.* This is because, up ahead, tucked away behind a little group of trees, is

The Doghouse.

This is a small house belonging to a very old couple called Lucinda and Henry. Lucinda and Henry live with their colossal family of dogs and cats. Lucinda and Henry love cats and

* Actually, for all I know they could be demanding to be told the answer to Three Down in today's crossword, or what today's football score was, or even what the ingredients were in the delicious dustbin stew they ate at lunch time, but until I learn to speak Cat, the true meaning of the sound that cats make will have to remain a mystery.

dogs more than anything else, which is just as well since they have ten dogs and twenty-seven cats, plus the biggest milk-bottle collection in the whole of Scotland.*

We stand on the doorstep, trying not to knock over any milk bottles and listening to the loud **barking** coming from behind the front door. In my arms, the Pumpkin wriggles and turns back into my little sister, round-eyed with wonder.

* Probably because twenty-seven cats can drink vast amounts of milk. Also, with ten dogs bounding around among twenty-seven saucers of milk, lots of milk will be spilled.

'WayWoo?' she whispers, as if hardly daring to believe that this might be where her missing dog is.

'Let's hope so, Daze,' says Vivaldi, leaning on the doorbell.

Eighteen:

A doggy bit

Immediately the barking grows ten times louder and is joined by the sound of something huge flinging itself against the door . . .

Ker – **thudda – thw**onk

over and over again

Ker – **thudDA – thw**onk

as if trying to break the door down

KeRRR – **thuDDaa – thWONK**kkk

and reach us.

Gulp. I know exactly what is making the door quiver on its hinges. I've *met* it. I barely escaped with my life last time.

'Bertie – DOWN – NO, don't jump up. Who's a GOOD boy? *NO!* Bertie, STOP THAT.'

That'll be Lucinda, trying her best to stop

the dreaded Bertie* battering down the door.

Ker – **tHUDDDa – tHWONKKKK**

Unfortunately Bertie never listens to Lucinda or Henry. Being a dog and weighing roughly one hundred kilos means you don't have to listen to *anything* other than the demands of your own stomach. It occurs to me that I would probably have suspected that WayWoof was here at The Doghouse a lot sooner if it hadn't been for Bertie. Bertie is such a monster that I'd

* Bertie. Think Hound of the Baskervilles crossed with the Abominable Snowman, dyed black, sprinkled liberally with fangs as long as your thumb, and with a stomach where its brain should be, and that's Bertie. If Bertie were a mountain, he'd be Everest; if he were a country, he'd be Russia; and if he were anything other than Lucinda and Henry's beloved pet, he'd be behind bars.

do just about *anything* to avoid being anywhere near him.

Ker – **thuDdda – thWONK**

Surely WayWoof wouldn't have . . . ? Tell me she didn't choose Bertie to be the daddy of her puppies? Surely she has more sense?

In between Bertie's assaults on the door, we can hear a metallic rattling sound: Lucinda turning keys and undoing latches and sliding bolts. Oh, heck. Here he comes . . .

'DOWN, BERTIE!' she bawls as the door bursts open and Bertie bounds through, crashes into Vivaldi and hurls himself out into the night.

Vivaldi **staggers**, thrown off-balance by having one hundred kilos of dog bouncing off her legs, but miraculously she doesn't fall into the doorstep glacier of milk bottles, and even more miraculously, she seems to find Bertie amusing.

'Here, boy,' she calls. 'Come here. Come and see me. Who's a *lovely* BIG boy, then?'

Is my dearest friend mad? She must be. I mean, when normal people catch sight of Bertie, they usually run *away*. Not Vivaldi. She waves her arms and runs *towards* him, showing every sign that she thinks this is a Good and Proper Thing to Do.

As does Bertie. The beast stops in mid-bound and reverses direction, a long whiplash of drool

spooling out behind him as he speeds towards
Vivaldi. The sight of that string of drool is quite
enough to make me pass out
with *horror*, but Vivaldi is made
of sterner stuff. When Bertie
and Vivaldi collide,
there's a flurry of
tail-wagging and
barking, then he
rolls over on his
back with all

four paws in the air and submits to having his tummy rubbed.

WOW. I'm seriously impressed by Vivaldi, beast-tamer. She must have a magic touch because Bertie is acting like a teddy bear, and in fact, if he weren't a dog, I could swear he'd be *purring* with pleasure.

Beside me, Lucinda is trying to stem the tide of dogs pouring out of the door, all of them curious to discover what Bertie has found. She jumps up and down, shrilling commands at the dog-pack, doing her best to bring them under control. Rooting in her pocket for a whistle or even a handful of dog biscuits, she shrieks, 'Down, BOYS. HEEL. Lie *down*. HEEL,' but the dogs pay her no attention at all. One by one, they make their break for freedom, having a quick *snuffle* at my bog-muddy legs, then a *sniff* at Daisy, before bolting off to sample Vivaldi.

There are dogs of all shapes, colours and sizes. Big dogs, small dogs, black, brown, white – even a pale pink one.

They **bark** and **yip** and pant, greeting these new humans Bertie has found, sniffing as they try to find out where we've come from. I check to see what Daisy is making of this mass dog-greeting and catch my breath.

Oh, my. Oh, *gosh*. Oh, YES!

Oh, *Daisy*. I want to rush to her side and hug her tight, to spin her round in a circle of delight because . . . there she is, eyes shining, both arms outstretched to welcome something that looks like the black shadow of a wolf . . .

. . . faint, but growing more solid, more dense . . .

And as a puff of wind brings a familiar smell drifting my way, I realize that at *last* we've found—

'WAYYYYYYYWOOOOOOOO!' Daisy buries her face in WayWoof's now-visible fur and clings on for dear life. Across Lucinda's garden, Vivaldi's head comes up from where she's been hugging Bertie the Beast and a **wild** grin appears on her face.

'YEEEE-HAWWWWW!' she yells. 'Way to *go*, Daze.' And abandoning Bertie, she runs over to greet our long-lost WayWoof.

For a moment WayWoof is completely surrounded by her humans, all three of us limp with the relief of having found her. We pat her, tell her how much we've missed her, how many places we've looked for her and, most of all, what a clever, beautiful and utterly loved-to-bits dog she is. In return, WayWoof rolls her long pink tongue all the way out of her mouth and halfway down her chest, pants with hot dog-breath . . . and lets rip with a really extra-special, eye-watering, clear-the-room . . . **cough**, gag, PHEW.

WayWoof's back.

Nineteen:

In The Doghouse

In the excitement of finding **WayWoof** we have managed to forget Lucinda. I cannot imagine *what* she must think Vivaldi, Daisy and I were doing, patting and stroking and cooing over an invisible something that only we can see. Normal humans can't see magical creatures like WayWoof, so Lucinda must think we are completely **crazy**, exclaiming over a dog that isn't there. However, although she can't *see* WayWoof, she can smell her. As she comes over to see what's going on, she coughs, blinks rapidly, and then peers at Daisy in dismay.

'Poor little mite,' she gasps. 'Does Baby need to go home to Mumsy and Daddykins for a nappy change?'

Daisy stops patting WayWoof and peers up at this strange old lady. 'No,' she says firmly. 'Wantit pup-pups.'

AAAARGH. The *puppies*. How could I have forgotten? Carried away with joy at WayWoof's reappearance, I completely failed to check her tummy. AaaaaaARGH. WayWoof is all skinny again. I can see her ribs. Oh, NO. Where are the puppies? What has she done with them? WayWoof? As if she can read my mind, she suddenly turns tail and streaks into The

Doghouse. At this, Daisy frowns and bawls, 'Way gone, PUP-PUPS?'

Fortunately, not only can Lucinda not see WayWoof; she can't really understand what Daisy is saying.

'Oh, dearie me, no,' she says. 'We don't have any puppy-wuppies here. Lots of dear little doggies, though. And simply heaps of pussycats. Would you like to see the pussycats, dear?'

Daisy's bottom lip pops out. **Uh-Oh**.

'No WANTIT pussycats,' she says. 'WANT pup-pups.' And before we can stop her, she spins round and bolts through Lucinda's front door.

Luckily Lucinda doesn't seem to mind Daisy gatecrashing The Doghouse. She's far more concerned with rounding up her dogs: she strides across her garden, yelling, 'BOYS! Come to Mummy. Here, BOYS. Naughty BOYS. Mummy will be *very* cross. HERE, boys.'

As she heads into the shadows, I spot the four guard dogs from Mishnish Castle, still magically transformed, floating across the sky, their balloon bodies and dangling leashes silhouetted against the moon.

They drift towards the faint glow of lights from the village, legs slowly pedalling in mid-air. From far away I hear Lucinda calling, 'Naughty boys. Come *down* at ONCE . . .'

Then the night and the distance swallow them all.

Vivaldi and I stand in the doorway of The Doghouse, uncertain what to do next. Vivaldi looks at me and bites her lip.

'I don't know what to do. Are you *sure* they're in there? The puppies, I mean.'

AaaaaRGH. I'm *almost* sure. About ninety-nine point nine nine nine per cent sure. Which is almost one hundred per cent. I take a deep breath and say, 'Yes. They *have* to be here. WayWoof is here – there are heaps of possible puppy-fathers here too, so . . .'

'We'll have to go in and look.' Vivaldi

groans and adds, 'But . . . but we can't just burst in and start opening doors. I mean, we hardly know Lucinda and Henry, and even if we did, we couldn't say, *Oh, hi, just ignore us as we turn your house upside down to find our invisible dog and her pups* – could we?'

She's right, but . . . none of this stopped Daisy. Daisy is in there right now looking for WayWoof and the puppies. Which gives us the perfect excuse to go inside too. I'm looking for my little sister, not her invisible dog. *Perfect.* Plus there are no guard dogs barking their heads off at the two strangers on their doorstep. All the dogs have headed off into the dark in pursuit of Lucinda and the dog balloons.

All the dogs except one. At least, I *think* it's a dog, though it is hard to tell. It's very black and exceedingly hairy, but there's something wagging at one end and there are two shining eyes gazing up at me from the other. A tiny pink tongue appears below the eyes and it grins up at me. Aha. It *is* a dog.

'Ahhhhhh, he's so sweet,' Vivaldi says, bending down to offer her hand to this tiny beast. 'I love Scottie dogs,' she adds, scrabbling around the little dog's neck to find its collar. 'Let's see who we've got here . . . right . . . he's called Macduff.'

At the sound of his name, Macduff wags his tail so much I worry that his legs might fall off. He's such a small, friendly bundle that it's impossible not to like him immediately. He runs round Vivaldi in circles until she stands up and says, 'Right. Lead on . . .' and Macduff scampers ahead of us into The Doghouse. He skids to a stop in the hallway and turns round as if to say, *Do keep up*, before bounding upstairs at an amazing speed considering how short his legs are.

Gulp. I hope this is all right. I feel as if we're trespassing – after all, this *is* Lucinda and Henry's house – but I *have* to find Daisy. Up we go, following Macduff's wagging tail. I can hear **loud** laughter and clapping coming from a television below, but from somewhere in the darkness at the top of the stairs there's a low, vibrating sort of hum.

Vivaldi is right behind me, **hissing** in my ear, 'What's that weird noise?'

'The sort of hum?' I ask.

'No – the breathing noise.'

'*Breathing?*' I gasp. 'I thought it was a fan or some kind of machine, or—'

We stop and listen. The noise is much louder. RrrrrrrrHrrrrrrHrrrrrr, it goes. What kind of thing breathes like that? Then, as we turn a corner, I almost laugh out loud. By the open door of a dimly lit bedroom I see about twenty cats, all purring loudly. RrrrrrrrHrrrrrHrrrrr, they go, ignoring us entirely, their attention fixed on something inside the room, all lined up as if guarding the doorway.

Stepping carefully over the cats, we tiptoe inside and . . .

Oh, **WOW**.

Oh my goodness.

I have *never* seen anything so gorgeous in

my life. Ahhhhh. I feel my eyes opening wider and wider as if they could *drink* in the sight of WayWoof and her tiny little puppies. Daisy is right beside them, almost *glowing* with happiness. She drags her gaze away from the puppies and peers at us briefly. 'Huss, Lil-Lil,' she mutters. 'Huss, Valdy. Pup-pups seeping,' and then she returns to giving the puppies her full attention.

WayWoof looks up at us, and then bends her head back down to nuzzle her two babies. She looks every inch a proud mummy, as she should be. Not wanting to be left out, Macduff picks his way past Daisy and, tail wagging frantically, joins in the nuzzling.

Vivaldi nudges me and whispers, 'He's the daddy.'

'How d'you know?' I whisper back.

'WayWoof would have bitten his head off if he wasn't. Female dogs are super-protective of their puppies.'

'D'you think she'll let us hold them?' I ask.

In answer, WayWoof rolls over and nudges one of her puppies towards me. I look at her, then look at the puppy, as if I'm asking her, *Can I? Are you sure you don't mind?*

WayWoof yawns widely and turns back to her other puppy as if to say, *Help yourself.*

So, very, very slowly and carefully, I pick the tiny creature up in my hands and hold it close.

Oh, my. The puppy opens its little mouth and yawns luxuriously. Its whiskers quiver with the effort and it gives a tiny squeak before closing its mouth again. It's *perfect*. It's like a wee crumpled cushion made out of pink and cream velvet. It's warm and soft and very much alive. And to my delight, it doesn't mind me holding it. It's the most gorgeous little animal I've ever seen.

Vivaldi reaches out and tenderly strokes the puppy's head with one finger. 'It's sooooo soft,' she whispers. 'Oh, clever, clever WayWoof. What beautiful babies you have.'

Macduff wags enthusiastically, as if agreeing with Vivaldi.

'Clever Macduff too,' I add, reaching out to pat him. As I do, I catch sight of Lucinda and Henry's bedside clock.

AAAAAAARGHHHHHH. It's *quarter past eight*. We're due home in fifteen minutes. Oh, *help*. I wish I could spend all night in Lucinda and Henry's bedroom gazing adoringly at WayWoof's puppies, but it's time to go. We haven't even got time to say thank you to Lucinda and Henry for allowing WayWoof to have her puppies on their bed. In fact, I'm hoping we don't meet either of our hosts on our way out, because then we'd have to explain just what we were doing upstairs in their house, on their bed, in the dark, with our invisible dog and her invisible puppies.

Fortunately the television is still on, so

nobody hears
us all tiptoeing
downstairs. First Macduff,
then WayWoof, Daisy and me
(with one puppy in my arms),
Vivaldi with the other puppy.
Followed by at least twenty
ecstatically *purring* cats. In
the living room Henry is watching
television, utterly oblivious to all the
excitement going on upstairs. Henry is very
old, and judging by the volume he has the
television turned up to, he is also rather deaf.

Macduff and WayWoof bid each other a fond farewell, wagging tails, rubbing noses and sniffing each other's bottoms. **Yeeeeurgh**. No matter how old or deaf I become, I'll *never* get used to dogs doing that. While WayWoof is saying goodbye, we hustle Daisy out of the front door and, whistling for WayWoof to follow, set off into the night.

Twenty:

My not-so-little sister

For such tiny creatures, WayWoof's puppies are surprisingly heavy. My arms are beginning to ache and I feel as if we're going slower and slower, the closer we get to home. WayWoof walks beside Vivaldi and me, looking up every so often to check that we're looking after her puppies properly. We're all flagging, especially Daisy, who is growing more and more cranky now that the excitement is over.

'Carry meeeeeeee,' she whines, dragging behind us.

Vivaldi and I stop to give our arms a rest and try to jolly her along. WayWoof immediately lies down. She's exhausted, poor thing.

'Not far now,' Vivaldi says. 'Let's count the

trees, Daisy. By the time we get to a hundred, we'll be home.'

'Not hunded. No wantit tees,' Daisy mutters, abruptly sitting down. '**C**a**rry meeee**,' and when neither Vivaldi nor I respond, she turns it up a notch: '**CARRY MEEEEEEEEE**.'

'Aw, come *on*, Daisy,' I groan. 'Give us a break. We're already carrying your blooming puppies *and* all the **Halloween** goodies—'

'**CARRRY MEEEEEEEEE**,' Daisy bawls, drumming her heels on the ground like a grumpy troll. '**CARRY MEEEEEEE, NO WANTIT WAAAAAAAAALK**.'

WayWoof peers at her and yawns, slumping onto the ground and closing her eyes as if to make Daisy go away. At this rate we're going to be *really* late home, and Dad'll be *really* cross, and I'll get the blame even though it's Not My Fault. *I* didn't magic up an invisible dog and carelessly let her run away to have puppies. I won't even be able to tell Dad what *really* happened because he won't believe me. It's not *fair*. This is *all* Daisy's fault, and what is she doing? She's lying on the ground, having a tantrum, waiting for *me* to sort it all out.

Suddenly I know how to get us all home in time. I fling myself down on the ground beside Daisy and let rip.

'NOOO WANTIT WAAAAAAAAAAALK HOME,' I roar, banging my legs and arms on the ground for emphasis. 'CARRRYYYY MEEEEEE, DAISEEEEEEEEE.'

WayWoof's head comes up and she shoots me a reproachful look, as if to say, *How could you? I thought you were such a sensible human child*; then she puts her paws over her ears and whimpers. I keep going, 'CARRRYYYY MEEEE,' but the thought occurs to me that Vivaldi might decide that my tantrum is the final straw. She might think that this was The Night Lily Went Too Far. For all I know, she may have already started to head for home. Poor Vivaldi has had to put up with a lot being friends with me: invisible gassy dogs, weird little witchy sisters—

'NO LIKEIT WAAAAAAALK!' comes a banshee shriek as Vivaldi flings herself down beside me and joins in. 'DAAAAAZE, CARRY MEEEEEE TOOOOO!'

I love Vivaldi. She never lets me down.

What a *friend*. What a *genius*. What a *brilliant* idea. What on earth—?

There's a *WHOOOOSH* as air rushes past my ears and a 'YEEEEARGHHH!' as I'm hauled up to the sky so fast my eyelids are pressed shut. Then I'm rocked from side to side as if I'm in a boat in a storm. I'm pressed up against something soft, below which I can feel a huge, pounding, thundering drumbeat. Where's Vivaldi? What is going on? I squirm round to look for her and immediately it all falls into place. Yeeearrghh. This has to be the weirdest spell Daisy has *ever* done.*

Way down on the ground below us, WayWoof is barking her head off. Can't say I

---

* You be the judge. For the title of Daisy's Weirdest Spell Ever, we have the following:
  • changing me into a slug
  • turning my head the wrong way round so that I was facing backwards
  • blowing me up like a human balloon and then letting me go *Pfffrpprrrrppp*
  • poking her fingers, hands and finally her *arms* up her nose and turning herself inside out.

I tell you, being a Witch Baby's big sister is Hard Work.

blame her. After
all, a gigantic
baby girl has
just appeared
from
nowhere,
picked up
the two

humans who were looking after her puppies and is now running off with puppies, girls *and* **Halloween** goodies. Vivaldi is clutched in a hand as big as a sofa and I'm squashed in the crook of an arm nearly the size of a bus. The thudding sound of a distant drum is my baby sister's heartbeat. Daisy is *enormous*. I look up at her huge mouth, smeared with acres of chocolate, beyond which are vast nostrils like

two big dark caves. Daisy is a big as a house. A BIG house. Yikes. An eyeball the size of a watermelon swivels down to stare at me. A gust of hot air blows across me as Daisy the Giantess says, 'NO WANTIT WALK? SEE DAISY RUN.'

And suddenly we're off, with WayWoof running behind.

Every step Daisy takes feels like a vast, soaring leap followed by a bone-jarring thud as her foot returns to earth. Amazingly enough, the puppies sleep through it all, barely moving so much as a whisker as we lurch and blunder through the trees towards home.

'LEFT!' I yell, and then, 'Watch out for the ROAD,' but Daisy ignores me completely. She's on a mission for home and she's going to head straight there, no matter what might be in the way.

'Slow dowwwwwwn,' I beg, but it's no good. Daisy is doing this **Her Way**, and we may as well settle back and enjoy the ride. I hope we don't meet anyone, because I suspect Daisy would squash them flat. Daisy, my not-so-little sister, the Spooky Steamroller. **Gulp**. That **Witch Baby**— WAAAARGH, DON'T *SQUEEZE* ME. Better not mess with *her*, eh?

It's very late and we do have school tomorrow, but Vivaldi and I are much too excited to sleep.

Apart from having my best friend for a sleepover, one of the best things about tonight was that when Daisy returned to her normal size, she forgot to do the same for the huge bag of **Halloween** goodies. **WOW**. We now have three chocolate coins the size of bicycle tyres, two bags of chilli-flavoured crisps as big as duvets and, weirdly, three pound coins the size and weight of manhole covers. We buried these under a pile of leaves since they were too heavy to carry and Vivaldi was sure the bank would never accept them as real money.

Daisy is fast asleep in her bed next door, WayWoof is back in her rightful place across Daisy's feet, and WayWoof's puppies are tightly curled up against their mum's tummy. I'm so relieved we managed to get them all home safely. Pheee-yew. What a night *that* was, but thank goodness it all ended happily. In fact, if you think about it, WayWoof didn't really run away; she just went elsewhere to have her puppies.

I look at Daisy, fast asleep in her bunny pyjamas. It's hard to believe that less than an hour ago this tiny tot was a deeply scary giantess. Daisy the Vast crashed through the woods in seconds flat and barrelled across our lawn; it was only when she realized that she wouldn't be able to fit through our front door that she turned back into a little girl.

Phew. Just in time. I had a moment of panic

when I really thought she was about to lift the
roof off our house to put Vivaldi and me inside
like she'd seen me do with my old doll's house.

Aaaargh. Imagine trying to explain *that* to Mum and Dad. *Er . . . remember we used to have an attic? And, um, about that gale blowing downstairs and the . . . er . . . gigantic hole where the ceiling used to be and . . .*

Luckily the puppies are as invisible as their mummy, but unlike **WayWoof's**, their **poo** isn't, even if, like most puppy-poo it doesn't smell yet.* Mum and Dad and Jack don't know that our invisible dog has not only come back but has also increased the invisible-dog-count in our house by two hundred per cent. However, Vivaldi and I have agreed that when the puppies are old enough to leave home, they're both going to live at Four Winds, Vivaldi's house. That way, Daisy, WayWoof and I can go and visit, but we won't have to look after them. Vivaldi reckons that I have quite enough magical creatures to care for without

---

* Pong-free poo? Yes, but only when the mammal in question is fed exclusively on its mother's milk. Add anything else into the diet and the poo will smell like . . . well, poo actually.

adding two invisible puppies to the menagerie.

'But won't your parents notice?' I ask, sawing off another slab of chocolate and popping it into my mouth.

'No way,' Vivaldi says through a mouthful of crisps. 'They never notice anything. Brahms once threw up in Mum's handbag and it took her *months* to work out where the smell was coming from . . .'

Eughhh. I swallow the chocolate rapidly and decide I don't want any more, but Vivaldi is unstoppable.

'And one night Dad had to change the tyre on the car and he didn't put the nuts or bolts or screws back on properly, and next morning he took us shopping, but he didn't notice that the wheel was making a really **weird** noise – the car was kind of lurching over to one side and we were driving down a hill through a wee village and people were waving and pointing at us and Dad thought they were just being dead friendly so he waved back . . .' Vivaldi is laughing so hard she can hardly carry on.

'What happened?' I ask.

'Trust me, Mum and Dad are *so* unobservant I could keep a hundred puppies and they'd never notice a thing. So – we were still driving through the village when we saw a car wheel roll across our path and head downhill, right in front of our car. Mum pointed it out to Dad, and they were both wondering where it could have come from, but it wasn't until a police car overtook us, pulled over and made Dad stop that we realized it was *our* wheel that had come off

completely and was racing us down the hill.'

Crikey. Vivaldi's right. With parents like
hers she could keep a zoo-full of WITCHY pets and
nobody would be any the wiser. My family aren't
much better. The only thing about WayWoof
they ever notice is her smell. Unfortunately,
once they've checked that Daisy's nappy isn't

responsible for the *evil* whiff, they all turn on *me*. I guess it's the price I have to pay for knowing a dog like **WayWoof**, but right now, I don't mind a bit. The puppies are *adorable*, and I can hardly wait till tomorrow to see them again.

'Vivaldi?'

'**Nnnngh**?'

Blast. She's falling asleep. I want to ask her what names we should give the puppies, but it would be cruel to wake her up. Besides, it's really up to Daisy to choose names, since WayWoof is her dog. I drift off to sleep trying to guess what names she'll come up with. I only hope that, whatever they are, they're not too *weird*.

Twenty-one:

Little beasts

'Vampie an' Boomstek,' Daisy mutters as I help her out of her coat and hang it on her peg in the school cloakroom. Next to us, Daisy's best friend, Dugger, bursts out laughing.

'Vampire and broomstick?' he shrieks, as if Daisy's just told him the best joke ever, then abruptly stops laughing and frowns. 'That's *silly*,' he declares, stomping off to the sandpit.

'*Not* silly,' Daisy says, tugging at my arm for support. 'My puppies not *silly*.'

'Er, no,' I say quietly, hoping nobody overhears. 'Not silly at all. You can call them whatev—'

'VAMPIE an' BOOMSTEK,' Daisy bawls, her face turning pink with the effort. Oh, great. *Everyone* in the school must have heard that.

Mum turns round and smiles. 'That was yesterday, darling,' she says. 'Yesterday was **Halloween**. We had vampires and broomsticks and bats and pumpkin lanterns *yesterday*. Today it's playgroup.'

Daisy sighs as if to say, *Yes, I know that*, and

280

then insists, 'Wantit Vampie an' Boomstek. Want PUPPIES.'

Mum nods patiently. 'Maybe in the springtime, pet. It's nearly winter now and it's no fun house-training puppies when it's cold outside.'

Aaaargh. Puppies? Next spring? *Real* puppies? No way. Not when we've already got two invisible magic ones. And their invisible magical mother too.

Daisy agrees. She glares at Mum and says, 'No wantit puppies. Want Vampie an' Boomstek. Wantit *my* puppies.'

Mum shoots me a despairing look – *What planet did you say your little sister came from?* – and then takes Daisy by the hand and leads her into playgroup. As they go, I hear her saying, 'What about a dear wee pussycat then, Daze? Ahhhhh. Or a bunny rabbit? Or even a guinea pig? That would be really sweet, wouldn't it?' I'm imagining how sweet WayWoof would find a bunny rabbit. Sweet? Possibly a little chewy too. Mum comes back out of playgroup, waves goodbye and heads for home. The cloakroom is filling up with my classmates, all of us able to hear Daisy's foghorn voice loudly insisting that BOOMSTEK and VAMPIE are the names of her PUPPIES. Oh, sigh.

'Ah used to have a rat,' Shane says, hanging up his jacket and changing into his indoor shoes.

'You *are* a rat,' Craig says, punching him on the shoulder and then dancing backwards out of range.

'We've still got *geese*,' Annabel says, slumping down beside Vivaldi and me and bending over to untie her laces. 'Daddy is furious. They attacked all his guests.'

'And they covered everyone's cars in goose . . . er . . . droppings,' Jamie adds, his face breaking into a huge grin. 'Actually, it was pretty funny. All those grown-ups in fancy dress running around flapping at the geese and trying to shoo them away.'

'Ah had a *frog* drop onto ma face,' Shane offers.

'A *frog*?' Yoshito covers her mouth as she giggles. 'Are you sure it wasn't a handsome prince?'

'What're you oan about?' Shane says; then the penny drops. 'Oh, *right*. Like in that fairy story? **Naw**. It was a frog, and ah can tell you it wisny handsome.'

'What about you, Lily?' Jamie asks. 'How was your **Halloween**?'

Er. *If only you knew*, I think. I'm almost tempted to tell him everything, just to watch his face change, but instead I tell him a tiny bit of the truth:

'Great. Full of *bats*, **spiders**, **DEMONS** and spooky eyeballs. We had a fantastic time, and we came home with more chocolate than we could eat, so I brought some in to share round.'

There's such a loud cheer at this. I'm slightly embarrassed, so I turn round to hang up my coat. When I turn back to face my classmates, Yoshito winks at me and says,

'I love your hat, Lily. I'm going to ask my fairy godmother to make me one too.'

Shane rolls his eyes. 'Fairy *godmother*? Ask her to make me rich and famous while you're at it.'

Yoshito smiles as if she's keeping a delicious secret to herself. 'You'll have to ask her yourself,' she says, then she runs off into the classroom.

As the bell rings to call us in, I think that although I like the idea of Yoshito having a fairy for a godmother, I'd far rather have a **Witch Baby** for a sister. You have to *ask* fairy godmothers for things; with Witch Babies all you have to do is wait and see what happens next.

Ae last Hiss

'She'll wear the pool out,' the Toad observed, sprinkling icing sugar over a chocolate raspberry meringue cake and hopping backwards to admire the result.

The Chin looked up from her knitting and sighed. 'You can't wear out *water*,' she snorted. 'How long has she been in there?'

'In the pool? **Pffff**. Three days? Four? I've lost count. And let's not forget that she'd already spent a week in the bath before you finally booted her out. *Honestly*. What a fuss. It was only a tiny little bit of Witch Baby **poo**—'

'A tiny little bit?' squawked the Chin. 'At least a *ton* of dinosaur doo-doo fell out of your precious little Witch Baby's bottom. Dis*gus*ting. I'm just thankful that *we* don't have to house-train our **Witch Baby**. How her parents can stand it I cannot imagine.'

In the silence a cloud of bubbles drifted past the kitchen window.

'Does she *have* to use quite so much bubble bath?' the Chin continued. 'Surely she must be clean by now?'

'At least while she's in the pool she's not stealing all our food,' the Toad muttered darkly, upending a tub of double cream over the chocolate raspberry meringue cake and adding some chopped toasted hazelnuts for added crunch.

'Stealing food? How can you blame her for giving in to temptation? Do you have to make such amazing food? Chocolate meringues with cream *and* hazelnuts? No wonder the poor Nose can't resist,' the Chin said, looking at the Toad's cake and shaking her head.

Crestfallen, the Toad began to carefully remove all the hazelnuts and cream with her tongue.

'We'll have to get her out of the pool,' the Chin said. 'She's going to turn into a **shrivelled** raisin if she stays in any longer. But then she'll just start eating us out of house and home. Perhaps you should put a lock on the fridge door?'

'Or I *could* stop cooking such lovely meals and we could return to eating stewed nettles and boiled rats like we used to,' suggested the Toad.

'Eurggghhh,' the Chin said, knitting faster. 'Don't do *that*. Isn't there a spell somewhere to turn greedy chocolate-stealing WITCHES into ones who only nibble salad?'

'Yes . . .' the Toad admitted. 'But if it's anything like the wart-removing spell that turned me into a toad, the Nose could well end up turning herself into a stick of celery.'

The Chin winced. Poor Toad. Nobody was ever allowed to mention the disastrous spell that had changed her into a toad. Perhaps they should put a lock on the fridge door, or . . .

'Nice hat you're knitting,' the Toad said, determinedly cheerful. 'Pretty colours too.'

The Chin nodded, adding another row of sea-green stitches to the beautiful hat she was making for Mr Harukashi's extraordinary daughter. A few days ago, a letter on pale sea-green paper had arrived for the Chin.

Fairy Oddmother (the letter said)
Thank you for the shoe. Papa is very happy. We are both looking forward to seeing you again soon. In the meantime it would be very nice if you would be so kind as to knit me a hat just like Lily's. Only in green, not red like hers.
Thank you

And beneath a row of little goldfish stickers was the signature:

'To read is to obey,' the Chin mutters, her
needles clicking busily.

By the
window, the Toad
is wondering what
to make for dinner;

outside, the Nose sees the first star of the evening appear in a darkening sky. Surely she's clean now? Her stomach gives a rumble of protest. What will the Toad have made for tea? she wonders. Time to head inside out of the cold.

witch baby and me

My life is in ruins. Here's why:

★ I have a baby sister called Daisy. She's not a *baby* baby, she's a *witch* baby.

★ Only *I* know this (that she's a witch baby). Everyone else thinks she's sweet and adorable.

★ Daisy's summoned up an invisible dog called WayWoof to be her pet. People can smell WayWoof but they can't see him – so they think the smell is me.

But worst of all is:

★ Mum and Dad have decided that we're moving house. To the far, far North of Scotland. Which means I'll never see my friends again!

978 0552 55676 7

witch baby and me at school

My New School
by Lily MacRae (aged nine)

★ I am the New Girl.

★ My only friend has got Mystery Spots
  and might be off school for weeks.

★ My little sister Daisy is starting
  playgroup . . . in the next-door classroom.

★ Nobody else knows this, but Daisy is a
  witch. That's witch as in, 'casts spells'.

★ How on earth can I keep her
  witchiness a secret?

978 0552 55677 4